IS THIS POSSIBLE?

APARNA MATHUR

INDIA • SINGAPORE • MALAYSIA

ISBN 979-8-88935-951-7

Contents

Introduction

This book is like a long-lost dream come true. I had never imagined that this day will ever come. Yay! I've done it!

Thank you, God, for all your blessings!

I would like to dedicate this book first and foremost to Dad, Late Kailash Mathur and Mum, Prabha Mathur, for always encouraging me.

My dearest brother, Vijay, has always been a great support.

I would like to thank my dearest sister, Rinku (Devika), from the bottom of my heart for her tremendous help in putting it all together.

Last but not the least, my inspiration for writing these stories is my dearest, darling nephew, Tanay.

I am grateful to all those who gave me positive encouragement.

The Eternal Love

Mary was beside herself with grief; she had always suspected that Elizabeth's marriage to Edward would end badly one day but had never imagined this.

She was inconsolable as her daughter lay dead right before her eyes! Elizabeth's husband, Edward, was grief-stricken at the wake, but behaved strangely, as though unmoved by all of this. All the neighbours present also noticed this strange behaviour. Could the loss of his wife be responsible for his strangeness?

Mary sat motionless in front of the body, while Edward paced up and down, a bit agitated and disturbed. He did strange things like fidget with the white sheet that covered his wife's body. He tried to cover her and seemed to discourage anyone who wanted to come close to her. Everyone present at the wake was a little sceptical, wondering if this was a natural death or if Edward had something to do with her untimely demise. But aside from his bizarre behaviour, there was little else to prove he was guilty. All eyes were on Edward who pretended to have lost his mind.

Mary was certain that it was in no way a natural death, as her dear daughter was full of life and always spoke positively about things. She had always wanted to live a long life. The prime suspect was her son-in-law, Edward, whom she had always disliked. Her daughter lay in front of her in a coffin, ready for her last journey. Mary looked blankly at her daughter's body, hoping that she would suddenly get up, run to her and give her a big hug as she always did. The grief-stricken mother had lost her only child. She sat there brooding as her mind went back in time.

Mary was the daughter of a rich real-estate dealer in London in the mid-forties and was brought up by governesses as she had lost her mother when she was just four years old. Her father never married again; he did not want his child to have a stepmother and was content to lead the life of a widower.

Mr John Wilson was a very strict man. He was tall, blue-eyed, and his golden hair was always tied in a ponytail, held in place with a silver band. He lived with his daughter in a huge mansion in a town called Dartford just outside London. The mansion was built on a four-acre plot of land by Mr Wilson who was considered a millionaire even in those days.

Wealth did not equal happiness in Mary's case. Her childhood was not a happy one. She was lonely as she saw her father very little and was only in the company of her governess and the many servants who helped run the household. Her father was mostly out of town on business trips and hardly spent time with his little daughter, Mary. But whenever he was in town, he made the most of it by being with his only child.

The death of her mother had left a vacuum in Mary's life. She remembered very little of her mother but grew up seeing her pictures and portraits that adorned the walls of the mansion. Time flew by and Mary grew up to be a very beautiful young girl. She was very elegant and sophisticated. All the boys in town swooned over her and hoped that they'd be lucky enough to marry her. She was the heartthrob of all of Dartford.

But her heart only yearned for Mark, the son of her governess, Mrs Simon. Mark's father was an officer in the British Army and was often away defending the country. Mark studied at Cambridge University and was a brilliant student. Mary's father was extremely fond of him too. He was very hardworking. Besides studies, he also worked for Mr Wilson as a finance controller and visited their house often. Mary was in love with Mark, but he was unaware of her feelings towards him.

Until one day, when Mark visited them as usual for some work, Mary ushered him to the backyard. Mark was alarmed, as she was the daughter of his employer, and his mother was also an employee of the family. He thought he had made some big mistake and that was why he was being summoned into the backyard to perhaps be reprimanded, or worse still, fired! As he went to the backyard, he was taken aback when Mary confessed her love for him! He could not believe his ears because he too had feelings for her but was afraid to express himself, fearing he'd lose his job.

Mary told Mr Wilson about her feelings for Mark, and he was only too happy to hear this, as he had always wanted Mary to marry a self-made man who would love and protect his daughter. Besides, he had known Mark since he was a little boy. He had always been very fond of Mark and immediately announced their wedding. He also requested Mrs Simon not to work with them anymore and accept Mary as her daughter-in-law.

Soon Mary and Mark were married. They had a blissful life, full of happiness and contentment. Six months passed by. One night at the dinner table Mary felt uneasy. She rushed to the bathroom and vomited. Mark and his mother were worried about her. The next day, Mary went to the doctor accompanied by her mother-in-law, and he announced that she was pregnant! On hearing this great news, they were in tears. Mary was overwhelmed. She told the doctor that she had suspected she was pregnant but wanted to be sure before telling the rest of the family.

Mr Wilson's happiness knew no bounds when he learned that he was soon going to be a grandfather. He told Mary that he regretted not spending time with her while she was growing up but would make sure he spent all his time with his grandchild.

Mary and Mark were, of course, thrilled to bits, as they were soon going to be parents. Mary had dreamed of mothering her child as she always craved for a mother's love herself. Mark wanted to work harder to give his child all the comforts of life.

Time flew and four months passed by peacefully. One day, as Mary was climbing down the stairs of her house she felt faint and before she could gather herself, she tripped and fell down the steps. The severe bleeding resulted in a miscarriage! Mary, Mark and the entire family were heartbroken and shocked. They were so looking forward to the pitter-patter of little feet.

Mary had to stay in the hospital for ten days as the blood loss had made her quite weak. Both Mark and Mary were very depressed. Mary felt emptiness and a deep sense of loss like never before. Mr Wilson could tell that this had deeply impacted his daughter. He asked Mark to perhaps encourage her to return to college to take her mind off this trauma. Mary decided to work for a charity instead, helping the poor and needy. It didn't heal her wound nor fill the void of losing her unborn child; but helping the less fortunate made her count her blessings.

The doctors had advised her not to conceive immediately after her miscarriage, as her body needed time to heal. Two years passed by, and she was sad and craved a child. Christmas was around the corner. It had snowed heavily, and the streets were white. There was a chill in the air. Once again, it was a white Christmas. A sad, white Christmas.

On Christmas eve, Mary felt a little tired and uneasy and the family thought that it was because of all the Christmas preparations. Three weeks passed and she continued to feel the same way but she didn't want to come to any conclusion, unless she was sure. Mary crossed her fingers and hoped she would be pregnant again. Mark took her to the doctor for a check-up, and, to their surprise and delight, she was pregnant!

This time, the doctor warned them that no risks should be taken because this was their last chance to become biological parents. Mark took no chances and asked Mary to stay with her father, as he would take excellent care of his daughter. Mrs Simon wasn't keeping well either so she was glad her daughter-in-law would get the support and assistance of the large staff at the Wilson household.

Mark requested Mr Wilson to take care of his wife until the birth of their child. Mr Wilson was happy to have the opportunity to spend more time with his daughter. He was always travelling when she was younger and rued not being around in her formative years. Mr Wilson took utmost care of his daughter. There were maids and nurses to attend to her; they were at her beck and call around-the-clock. Mary was advised complete bed rest for at least the next four months.

Time passed very slowly, but the bond between father and daughter grew stronger and Mary was happy to see her father's softer and innermost side. He was a very caring and warm father and loved his daughter more than anything else in the world. Mark often came to meet his wife and on occasion, spent the weekend with them.

Mary's health improved. She was allowed to move a little, but never when alone. She was not allowed to use the stairs. She had put on a little weight, which the doctor thought she needed, as she was underweight. She kept herself busy by reading as many books as she could lay her hands on and did a lot of knitting for the baby. Days passed by quickly and her due date was nearing. The couple's anxiety grew.

Two days before the due date, Mary's water broke, and she was rushed to the hospital. She was in labour for twenty hours. She had excruciatingly painful contractions. Her father, mother-in-law and husband eagerly awaited the arrival of the baby. Their anxiety grew but there was nothing to do but wait. Mark tried to comfort his wife, while his mother assured a rather worried Mr Wilson that all would be well.

At last, they heard a musical cry from the operation theatre; the nurse came out announcing that it was a baby girl. On hearing the news their joy knew no bounds. A mini-Mary! They had all waited for this news for two long and difficult years.

The baby was eight pounds, with lovely blue eyes, thick golden hair and a beautiful complexion. They named her Elizabeth! As Mary took her in her arms for the first time, seeing this wonderful gift from The Almighty made all her pain vanish. She was in tears as she held her little angel close to her. They were all happy and relieved that everything had gone smoothly. Finally, Mark and Mary were proud parents of a beautiful daughter named Elizabeth.

The doctors advised Mary not to strain too much and take care of the baby, and more importantly, herself. Life had suddenly changed for the whole household. Everything revolved around the child. Mark's routine was turned upside down as he spent most of the day at home watching his baby sleep. They all took turns holding the baby, even though she slept most of the time! She was just too precious.

A fortnight passed and a tragedy struck Mark's family. His mother, Mrs Simon, passed away; she had been ailing for quite some time now. Mr Simon had also passed on a year ago, killed on duty. Mary was now alone with no elders in the family to support or guide her.

Mr Wilson suggested that they should move in with him. He was growing old and wished for some company, and of course, wanted his daughter and granddaughter to live with him. Mark had great respect for him and his wishes were their command, so they shifted to the mansion.

Elizabeth was growing fast and just like that it was time for her to go to school. Mr Wilson thought it would be a good idea if a tutor came home to teach his granddaughter, and Mark as usual agreed to whatever Mr Wilson desired. But Mary put her foot down and insisted firmly that her daughter should go to school, socialize with other children of her age and experience all phases of life on her own.

Elizabeth grew up as a princess in her grandfather's house. She had a strong bond with Mr Wilson. Many years passed by and soon Elizabeth was eighteen; it was time for her to go to college. She had grown into a beautiful, dainty, intelligent, but very stubborn girl as she was really spoiled by her father and grandfather. Her mother was extremely fond of her, but she wanted Elizabeth to be disciplined and get ready for marriage and face the world.

Elizabeth's best friend throughout school was Jane. Jane was a triplet. Her twin brothers were Jack and John and they all looked alike. While they were still in school, Jane's family had to move overseas to Italy. Even though the girls had got separated, they kept in touch through letters. Elizabeth missed Jane a lot as they used to share everything with each other. They were the closest of friends even though they came from very different backgrounds.

It was the first day of college, and Mr Wilson insisted on accompanying his granddaughter to college! Mary could not dissuade him. Elizabeth was very nervous on the inside as she was a shy girl. As their car entered the college grounds her nervousness grew, but she did not want to show it, as her grandfather would take her right back home! As she got out of the car, she saw a trio coming towards her, beaming and waving wildly. She jumped with happiness upon recognizing them. She was reunited with her beloved Jane and her twin brothers. She couldn't believe her eyes!

With them was a rather good-looking boy. Elizabeth wondered who he was. She hadn't seen the triplets in so long and was relieved that she would have some familiar faces in this overwhelmingly huge college! Her nervousness disappeared, knowing she would no longer be lonely. Jane and Elizabeth had so much to catch up on, that they had forgotten about the boy who stood beside them.

Jack nudged Jane to introduce the strapping young man to Elizabeth. Jane introduced the good-looking boy as Edward, their cousin from Italy who had come with them to study there. He was staying in the boys' on-campus residence with Jack and John.

Soon everyone got busy with college life, projects, and work. They got into a routine. The girls hardly met the boys as they were busy with their own projects and college clubs. Jane and Elizabeth of course always made time to gossip with each other! But they rarely saw Edward. Elizabeth enquired about him, but Jane said that he was involved in many of the college's societies and clubs so had little time to socialize with his cousins.

Then came the event all the newcomers looked forward to: The fall ball! Jack and Elizabeth were planning to attend it together, as they had liked each other right from childhood and this friendship seemed to be blossoming into love! Elizabeth wanted to be with Jack as much as she could, but it was not always possible.

To her surprise, Edward actually spoke to her and asked her to be his date to the dance! It was the first time he had paid any attention to her at all. She was about to politely decline because she was planning to go with Jack but Jane intervened and said, "Jack can't make it, Elizabeth! Go with Edward. Here's a note from Jack."

She was very disappointed as she read the note and agreed to go with Edward. All eyes were on Elizabeth at the ball, as she looked ravishing in a pink evening gown and with her, was the good-looking Edward. The dance floor was all set to rock. Edward could not take his eyes off Elizabeth even though her eyes searched only for Jack, who she hoped would surprise her. But he was out of town that evening, and she missed him terribly.

Edward took Elizabeth's hand and gracefully led her to the dance floor; the music began, and they started dancing. Elizabeth noticed that he was an excellent dancer and a thorough gentleman. Meanwhile, Edward had fallen head over heels for Elizabeth that night, completely floored by her beauty and her superb dancing skills. He was in love with her!

But to Elizabeth, he was just a friend and Jane's cousin. That night, Edward couldn't sleep, thinking of the lovely and memorable evening he had had. On the other hand, Elizabeth was so exhausted that she slept like a log.

Jack often took Elizabeth out for dinners and dances and her family was extremely fond of him. They knew that Elizabeth and Jack liked each other. Mary and Mark had always thought of him as their future son-in-law and Mr Wilson would do anything to see his granddaughter happy. She meant the world to him.

Jack was a charming young man, and his family was wealthy. While they were in Italy, he worked many jobs even though his family had money and property. His family also gave him more importance, being the eldest of the children. Mark, being a self-made man himself, appreciated that Jack had not just come into money but worked hard to earn his own. Jack and Elizabeth became closer. The whole college knew that they were madly in love with each other. On the other hand, Edward felt miserable as he was in love with Elizabeth too!

Every week there were opportunities to volunteer on campus so students could gain some sort of 'real world' experiences. One week, Elizabeth was to oversee the medicines at the college clinic. One afternoon, as Jane and Elizabeth were leaving the college, Edward shouted her name and she stopped. He asked her for some medicine, and she noticed that he looked very pale. Before she could ask him what medicine he needed, he passed out! With the help of some other students, the duo put him in the car and took him to their house. It was the least she could do to help her cousin, Jane thought.

The doctor was summoned and after Edward was examined, he informed them that it was nothing to worry about; it was just the flu, and he would be fine in a week. Elizabeth visited Jane's house twice to see Edward; it was an excuse to see Jack too. It was an open secret, but his parents did not appreciate them meeting each other so often before marriage.

The ten-day mid-term break rolled around soon. Elizabeth's aunt, Martha, Mark's sister, had invited all of them for a vacation but they could not go because of prior commitments. However, they decided to send Elizabeth instead as it would be a good change for her. Martha had a daughter, Sarah, who was just a year younger than Elizabeth. She was very fond of Elizabeth, but Elizabeth found her a bit annoying. Regardless, she was very fond of her aunt and wanted to visit her in the countryside, which was just an hour's drive from their house.

Sarah too was the only child of Martha and Nicholas They had built a farmhouse in the countryside and lived there for years now. Sarah was short and chubby. She was a good-natured, affectionate girl. Elizabeth and Sarah had often played together in their childhood.

Even though she found her a tad bit annoying at times, Elizabeth was fond of her cousin and looked forward to meeting her.

As she neared their farmhouse, she saw Aunt Martha waiting at the door. Elizabeth waved to her aunt who was thrilled to see her niece after so long. They both greeted each other very warmly and Martha took her inside. Sarah was in her room. Upon hearing that her cousin had arrived, she came thumping down the stairs as she was quite fat. Nicholas was at work so Elizabeth didn't see her uncle until much later that evening.

After dinner, Sarah took Elizabeth to her bedroom and then the cousins began to chat. Elizabeth wondered why Sarah was so keen that they should have a secret chat. Finally, Sarah spilt the beans and told her cousin that she was in love with a very good-looking boy, and he too was mad about her. She intended to marry him after finishing college. Elizabeth got very excited and wanted to tell Sarah how she too had found a special someone in Jack but did not get the opportunity as Sarah went on about her love interest.

Elizabeth then asked Sarah if she had a picture of her boyfriend. The latter blushed and took out a worn-looking photograph from under her pillow and showed it to Elizabeth. To Elizabeth's utter shock, it was the picture of *her* boyfriend, Jack! She could not believe her eyes; she rubbed them and looked again, and it was unmistakably Jack.

Her face dropped and she sat there, motionless. Sarah wondered what had happened and asked Elizabeth why she looked as white as a ghost! Elizabeth did not want to hide anything from her cousin and told her the whole story about Jack. Now it was Sarah's turn to be shocked. Both were heartbroken and felt cheated. Elizabeth realized that he had two-timed both girls. They were in tears but at the same time they were furious about Jack's behaviour. Elizabeth told Sarah not to mention it to anyone; she would teach him a lesson when she returned to college! Sarah, still heartbroken, agreed with her cousin.

Soon the break was over, and it was time for Elizabeth to return home. She was really hurt as she had loved Jack a lot and wanted to marry him, but now she was only angry about being cheated on. Sarah had cautioned Elizabeth against telling Jane anything as they were best friends. Sarah was hurt but not as much as Elizabeth was since she had only recently met Jack. However, she was furious on Elizabeth's account, since Jack had known her since they were children. That scum! Elizabeth felt a sense of relief after having this heart-to-heart with Sarah, as they had never been very close. At the same time, she was shattered and part of her did not want to return to college.

As she reached home, her grandfather was eagerly waiting for her and so were her parents. They had missed her a lot as she had been away for almost ten days. That night, the family once again had dinner together, and Mr Wilson noticed that Elizabeth didn't seem like herself. He asked her what the matter was but she said that she was just tired and wanted to sleep.

After dinner, all of them retired to their bedrooms. Elizabeth sat in her room wondering how a man she had loved could betray her. It was a total shock to her, and she was deep in thought when she heard a knock on her door and was surprised to see her grandfather's kind face! He was worried and could make out from her face at dinner that there was something amiss. He asked her what the matter was. She smiled and told him that there was nothing wrong, but he was adamant and insisted on knowing the truth.

After much coaxing, Elizabeth finally told him everything and broke down. He was furious and upset seeing his grandchild like this. Mr Wilson told his granddaughter not to mention it to anyone, not even to her parents as they would react impulsively. She should also keep her distance from Jane who was not only her best friend but also Jack's sister.

That night, Elizabeth had trouble breathing. Her wheezing and coughing worried Mr Wilson, so he called the doctor. He promptly informed them that it was an asthma attack, and it could have been worse had he not been informed in time. He advised her to quit smoking and take it easy because stress and anxiety are well-known triggers. She shouldn't aggravate the situation.

Elizabeth's parents were in a state of panic and wondered why this had happened. Mr Wilson, who knew the cause, assured them that their daughter would be fine and there was nothing to worry about. But Elizabeth did not feel comfortable lying to her parents, so she blurted out the truth to them. Needless to say, they were shocked. Jack seemed like such a nice boy!

On hearing the news of Elizabeth being unwell, Jack and Jane rushed to see her at her house, but to their surprise they weren't permitted inside, on strict instructions from Mr Wilson, as he did not want his granddaughter to be hurt further. Jack was surprised that for the first time, he and his sister were not welcome in the mansion but did not know why.

A week passed by and Elizabeth began to feel better. She was allowed to resume college but was not keen to return to the campus, as she would have to face the triplets. But with the support and encouragement of her family, she gained strength and dared to face every hurdle.

After his classes, Edward greeted her warmly and asked after her health. She was glad to see him, a friend she hoped she could trust after the people she thought she knew well, had betrayed her! He invited her for a cup of coffee in the cafeteria and she readily agreed. She enjoyed his company and needed it right now. As they entered the cafeteria, they saw the triplets sitting with some other friends. As they saw Edward and Elizabeth, Jack almost jumped out of his seat and rushed towards

Jane. He attempted to embrace her but to his shock, Elizabeth raised her arm and slapped him as hard as she could! Her eyes blazed with anger and tears streamed down her flushed face.

The whole cafeteria was stunned at what they had just witnessed. Elizabeth, still seething, told the gathering what Jack had done and how he had betrayed not only hers but her entire family's trust and ruined years of friendship! Jack and his siblings were completely taken aback and the whole crowd looked on in shock. Edward stood beside Elizabeth silently, disgusted and ashamed of his cousin's behaviour, hardly able to fathom how anyone could stoop so low! Of all people, Jack, his cousin!

Jane stood there feeling very guilty. She admitted to Elizabeth that she knew about Sarah, but since she thought it was a passing interest did not tell her best friend. Now it was Jane's turn to face Elizabeth's wrath! She yelled at her for hiding the truth and keeping mum about Jack's abominable behaviour. There was no excuse for breaking two hearts. Jane tried to apologize but Elizabeth had had enough and vowed she would never forgive them for betraying her. She was completely shattered and for a moment felt there was nothing more to look forward to in life.

That day was horrible for the whole college as news of the betrayal and heartbreak spread like wildfire. Everything seemed to come to a standstill. All eyes were full of scorn and contempt for Jack and Jane as well…and pity mixed with mirth for Elizabeth. How could she have been so naive?

Edward could not see Elizabeth in such a state and was ashamed that he was related to the trio. She was going through a very bad phase and he realized that she needed a friend more than anything else at this time. She had lost trust in people and relationships; it would be an uphill task to get her to trust anyone as a friend. After being humiliated in front of the entire college, the trio decided to leave the university, never to be seen again!

Meanwhile, Edward extended his friendship to Elizabeth, but she was very afraid as he was Jack's cousin. Edward assured her that he had nothing to do with them as he was disgusted by Jack's behaviour. She did not trust anyone, but Edward made sure that he did not speak or do anything that would hurt her feelings in any way.

Time flew by and Edward and Elizabeth became good friends. He shared everything with her, even the smallest details of his life, and she appreciated his openness with her. As the days passed by she started liking him for his honesty and truthfulness. Though she was reserved and had gone through some tough times, she also started sharing things with Edward but was still uncertain whether she was doing the right thing.

Edward's kindness and warmth helped heal the wounds caused by Jack. Elizabeth slowly forgot the pain of her past. She respected him and was grateful for his friendship but deep down she always feared that he too might leave her and was unable to trust him fully, though she continued to share things with him.

During their many conversations, he revealed to her that he did not come from a wealthy family like hers. Edward also told her that he had had a girlfriend, but things did not work out between them because they realized that it was just a passing phase. Elizabeth was pleased that Edward shared intimate details of his past with her.

After a few months of their friendship, Elizabeth invited him for her birthday, and he was thrilled to bits. Upon reaching the Wilson mansion, Edward shivered with nervousness, as he had never seen such a big house in his life and had never been to such a classy and sophisticated party. The whole mansion was decorated with all sorts of flowers, drapes, and canopies and was lit up as though it was Christmas. Elizabeth was happy to see him. He presented her with a lovely bouquet. She appreciated his simplicity and was also pleased that he did not waste money on expensive gifts to impress her. She introduced Edward to her family. They knew he was Jack's cousin, but they did not mention it.

Mary did not show any inclination towards him, and many questions came to her mind. She was worried about her daughter, because of what she had gone through and just wished that no one would ever hurt her again.

Mr Wilson and Mark spoke to Edward very warmly, and Elizabeth introduced him to all her friends as her close friend. All the girls at the party swooned over him, as he was quite the looker, but his eyes were only on Elizabeth. He longed to tell her how much he loved her. The party went on till the wee hours of the morning and most of Elizabeth's friends stayed overnight, but Edward went back to the hostel.

Months later, as Elizabeth and Edward were crossing Park Road one day, Edward saw a car speeding towards them even though the light was red! He rushed to her, grabbed her arm and pulled her to the sidewalk just as the car zigzagged past where they had been walking! Elizabeth was shocked and stood motionless, holding Edward tight; had it not been for him she would have been dead! She did not know how to thank him, but he modestly brushed it away saying it was his duty to save her. Afterall, he was her friend. He offered to drop her home as she was quite shaken.

As they approached the mansion, Mary saw that her daughter's face was white as a sheet! She asked Elizabeth what the matter was. After gathering her composure, Elizabeth told her mother everything. Mr Wilson, who was standing at the door, overheard them and was stunned and grateful to Edward for saving their precious Elizabeth's life. They couldn't stop thanking him. Mr Wilson told Edward that he had not only saved Elizabeth's life, but three other lives too.

By doing something he thought was trivial, Edward had won over the family's support, but he was unsure if

Elizabeth would give him her heart. He did not impose himself on her but was happy to be a close friend. She began trusting him but was uncertain if she liked him more than just a friend. Meanwhile, he was madly in love with her but was too scared to tell her. Elizabeth thanked him every day, as she was indebted to him, but he held his tongue. He did not dare to express himself; what if she said yes because she felt obligated to do so, not because *she* really felt the same way? He didn't want her to say anything she didn't truly feel.

A few weeks later, Edward did not come to college one day. Elizabeth thought that perhaps he had decided to take a day off. Four more days passed by and there was still no sign of him. Elizabeth got a little worried and inquired about him with his hostel roommate. To her surprise, he told her that Edward was down with a high fever and would probably not return to college for another week. The thought of not seeing Edward for a whole week made Elizabeth very sad. She couldn't explain this sadness; all she knew was that she wanted to see him and couldn't bear to be away from him. She started missing him terribly.

Girls were not allowed in the boys' residence unless they were related. The days seemed boring and empty without Edward. She could not hide her feelings for him. Neither could she tell anyone about how miserable she felt without him.

At home, she seemed lost and even at dinner she hardly touched her food. Mr Wilson noticed the sadness on her face and the emptiness in her eyes. On questioning her, she told him about Edward's illness, and his absence from college for another week. Hearing this, he smiled mischievously, recognizing the telltale signs of young love! Her darling granddaughter was in love; her eyes said it all. He comforted her by saying that Edward would soon be fine and resume college.

Ten days passed by and finally, the sun seemed to shine for Elizabeth. That morning, as she reached college, she saw Edward waiting for her at the door and her happiness knew no bounds; everything seemed so nice and wonderful again. He looked pale and weak, but they were happy to see each other. Her face was lit with happiness, and she wanted to be with him all day. He too wanted to spend time with her as he had also missed her a lot.

That evening, Edward gathered all his courage and asked Elizabeth if she had missed him even a little bit. To his surprise and delight, she poured her heart out to him, and later that evening, he proposed to her, as he was now sure her feelings for him were truly hers and not a result of any obligation. His happiness knew no bounds and they spent the rest of the evening holding each other's hands and looking into each other's eyes. It was a memorable day for both. Elizabeth deserved all the happiness.

They decided to get married only after finishing college. Edward wanted to talk to her parents, but Elizabeth was sceptical and told him that they should wait and not be hasty. But he was keen that they should talk to them at the earliest; he wanted to meet them that very day. She wanted some time, but he was adamant. That evening, he accompanied her to the mansion, and they both broke the news to her parents and Grandpa Wilson, who was thrilled! Both men agreed immediately but Mary had her doubts. She was very upset over the hasty decision to get married. As soon as Edward left, she did not mince her words and gave her daughter a piece of her mind!

Elizabeth was not as aggressive as her mother. She meekly tried to convince her of her love for Edward and how she had thought long and hard about this. It wasn't a passing phase or a teenage infatuation! She really did love him! She also reminded her mother that he was the one who had saved her life without any ulterior motive. He had never ever tried to be anything more than just a good friend.

But her mother was adamant. She thought this was a facade, an act to win the family over. He was, after all, aware that she was the sole heiress to the huge family wealth. Elizabeth was persistent too. She had her mother's stubborn streak and wouldn't budge.

"I will marry him, come what may," she told her mother.

Mary reluctantly agreed. She firmly believed it was not a suitable match; he was from abroad, a different culture, a completely different world and worse, he was Jack's cousin. The Jack they had all trusted. The Jack who had betrayed her daughter's trust. Her trust. She couldn't forgive or forget any of that. But she was helpless. The men of the family thought that Elizabeth and Edward made a fine pair and should get married as soon as possible!

In a few weeks, the whole college knew about their relationship; it was hot news and spread like wildfire. They were the talk of the town, as Elizabeth was beautiful, came from an aristocratic background and was loved by all. She was also very popular because of her kind and down-to-earth nature. Everyone thought that Edward was the luckiest man on earth.

Three years passed by. The couple finished college and Edward wanted to study further, but Mr Wilson, who was now ailing, wanted to see them married while he was still around! Edward could continue studying even after they were wed. Grandpa Wilson hoped they would consider this to be his last wish.

Edward's family came down from Italy for the wedding. Both families met each other and thankfully liked each other, which was so very important for the couple. A date was picked. Invitations were sent out. Everyone was thrilled, except for Mary. She had a strange feeling that this marriage wouldn't last long.

She had liked Edward, but not as a future son-in-law. She made a last-ditch attempt to perhaps convince her daughter to change her mind, but in vain. Elizabeth was determined to marry Edward. Mary had to agree to her daughter's wishes and hoped The Almighty would watch over them. With this comforting thought, she began to prepare for her daughter's trousseau.

It was a grand wedding and the entire town was witness to what could have been easily labelled the wedding of the century! After the ceremony, Mr Wilson gifted his granddaughter a beautiful silken scroll. This was an unusual present. Elizabeth was a bit surprised and looked at him questioningly. He smiled and told her to open it. She unrolled it and to her surprise, it was his will! He had given everything to his granddaughter and her husband Edward, except the farmhouse and some cash which he had kept for his daughter. Elizabeth's eyes welled up.

"But this is too much. I cannot accept this, Grandpa," she said through her tears.

Mary thought that her father had made a big mistake by including Edward's name in his will. He would ruin her daughter's life, she was sure of it, but unfortunately, she was helpless and continued to pray for the best.

Mr Wilson later explained to Mark and Mary that he had put Edward's name in the will because his gut said that he was a good man and now was the husband of their beloved child and should be wholeheartedly accepted by the entire family.

The wedding festivities were over, and the newlyweds left for their honeymoon to Europe. The Wilson mansion was quiet and sad. Mr Wilson's health seemed to be deteriorating. The doctor told Mark and Mary that it was just a passing depression more than anything else and he would be fine once his granddaughter returned home!

Sure enough, a month passed by, and the mansion was decorated once again! This time it was to welcome the newlywed couple returning from their honeymoon. Mr Wilson's health indeed improved, he was very excited, as he would soon see his darling granddaughter! Mary and Mark, despite Mr Wilson's protests — he wanted them to stay with him at his mansion — presented them with a beautiful villa where they could start their married life, very close to their own house.

After returning from their honeymoon, Edward told everyone that he wanted to study further and pursue a degree in law. This pleased his in-laws, especially Mary, who was convinced he would turn out to be a freeloader.

The next few years passed by happily. Edward had become a well-known lawyer because of his hard work. He had travelled around the world, because of his cases and clients. His business as a lawyer was well established, and he gave his wife all the luxuries and comforts he could. He loved her dearly and she loved him deeply. It truly was a match made in heaven.

One day, Edward told her that he would be out of town for four, maybe five days. If she liked she could stay at the Wilson mansion, as he worried about leaving her alone because of her asthma attacks. She told him not to worry. She would be fine, but surely, she would visit them every day. Elizabeth spent the following day at the mansion. After a lovely day spent with her family, she returned home late at night. Little did she know that it was to be her last. Their housekeeper found her dead the next morning.

Mary's thoughts were interrupted; she returned to the stark reality that her child was no more. A hand on her shoulder made her turn around. It was her husband, Mark. He had just returned from the hospital after admitting Mr Wilson, who had had a severe heart attack and was now critical after hearing about the death of his darling granddaughter.

Edward had called them with the dreadful news in the wee hours of the morning. He was away but his housekeeper had managed to reach him, and he had rushed back home hoping against hope that the housekeeper was mistaken. But it was not to be so.

Both the parents were shattered and had to gather the courage to bid a final farewell to their only child who now lay motionless before them. The hardest moment of their lives had come, the burial of their beloved child. They were going to put her to sleep for the very last time. This was the irony of life.

Edward also broke down as he put the last shovel of mud on the casket. Both parents somehow knew that it was not a natural death, and their eyes were on Edward. He knew he was being looked at with suspicious eyes, but was helpless, as he could not convince them in any way. He loved Elizabeth dearly, but no one would believe him at this stage.

Mr Wilson could not bear this great loss and passed away soon after Elizabeth's death. It was yet another other blow to the already-grieving family! Mary and Mark were left to console each other. Edward came to visit every day, but they did not think much about his presence. The parents were helpless as they had no evidence to prove that Edward was responsible for their daughter's death. They wished that their beloved child would return to life and tell them that she hadn't died a natural death and that her husband had murdered her!

But the dead don't come back! The doctors had told them that it was a severe asthma attack that had led to her untimely death. They refused to believe the doctors and knew in their hearts that something was amiss.

A fortnight passed by. One night, Edward and his in-laws were having dinner at the mansion, when suddenly the room brightened, and the candle flame flickered rapidly. It was rather alarming! There was no breeze, no window or door open and no draft in the very stuffy old dining room. It scared them. Suddenly, they heard a whisper. They shivered with fear and looked around expecting someone to have broken into the house! Who could it be? The whisper grew louder until it was a very familiar voice! It was Elizabeth's!

They looked around wildly not comprehending what was happening! Edward looked up to see the old chandeliers gently rocking. The Voice spoke. It was Elizabeth. She told them not to be scared and that her spirit couldn't leave. She wasn't happy. She needed their help in punishing the person responsible for her death!

Both parents, their hearts beating rapidly, had tears in their eyes and angrily looked at their son-in-law, who tried to hold back his tears. To their shock, Elizabeth's spirit told them not to accuse Edward of anything! He was innocent. The one responsible for her death was none other than Jack!

But how could this be true? Mary thought he had left for good and was far away from their lives. They were in disbelief. This only happened in the movies. Not in real life and not in their life! They couldn't believe that their daughter was present and speaking to them. Elizabeth's spirit narrated the whole story to them.

"That night when I returned home, it seemed strange; the housekeeper was nowhere to be found and the entire house was in darkness. I switched on the lights and went to the living room. A man sat in the chair, his back towards me. Edward wasn't in town so who could it be?"

The Voice paused. Edward looked around. The candle flickered steadily. Brighter than ever. The Voice continued. "He turned around and I was shocked to find Jack right before me! The sight of him made me angry and it brought back all the wrong he had done to our family. I asked him why he had broken into my house. He said nothing but smiled. It was an evil smile and it scared me. He told me that he had been keeping an eye on us for months and was waiting for an opportunity to get me alone so that he could make his move. He knew that Edward travelled often and was away that night on work. He wanted to avenge the day I had humiliated him. He approached me. He said he would teach me a lesson. I was so afraid, Mother. I slapped him hard, and he grabbed a hold of my wrist so tight that it hurt!"

Tears streamed down Edward's face. He looked heartbroken. Elizabeth continued. "I did not know what to do, so I bit him hard, freed my wrist and ran upstairs to my room. I could barely breathe! Gasping and panting, I shut the door behind me. Still coughing, I made my way to the nightstand to reach for my inhaler! This was one of the worst asthma attacks I had had in a while. My fear probably made it worse! As I grabbed my inhaler and brought it close to my mouth, Jack barged into the room, and lunged at me, knocking the inhaler out of my hands. He pushed me onto the bed, let out a loud laugh and picked the inhaler off the ground. I was doubled over coughing, gasping for breath. He didn't budge. I begged him, rasping and gasping for air. He just stared at me menacingly, his eyes ablaze! I begged and pleaded. He put forth a condition, but I wouldn't give in. I would not sleep with him. I fought. I coughed. But didn't give in to his demands. My lungs couldn't take it anymore. I died soon after."

Mary broke down. Edward was inconsolable. He had never felt so helpless in his life. He felt as though he was responsible for his wife's death. It was he who had left her alone so often. He should've been more present. He was deep in thought when the Voice spoke again.

"My soul cannot leave. I cannot rest until justice is served. You must find the inhaler. It will that prove Jack committed the crime and bring him to justice!" There was sadness in her voice.

Mary and Mark looked at Edward who was now sobbing uncontrollably. For the first time, Mary put her arm around him and tried to console her son-in-law. For the first time, she realized her dead daughter was right. Edward cared deeply about her and loved her with all his heart. But alas, it was too late. And they had to face their grief together.

Suddenly, Edward remembered the housekeeper telling him that fateful morning about Elizabeth lying dead on the bed. She had mentioned to him that the inhaler was missing. Edward, in his state of shock, hadn't given it any thought, but now it seemed like that inhaler was a critical piece of evidence! He tried to wipe his red eyes with his sleeve, vowing to take Jack to the gallows.

He ran upstairs to their room. He could feel the void left behind by his wife. He hadn't been able to touch anything in the room. It was much too painful. The staff had also been instructed to leave everything as is. He looked around. There was no sign of the inhaler. The room looked like it had seen quite a scuffle. The sheets were still ruffled, the nightstand drawer still open. The rugs were crumpled, and there, by the corner of the bed, tucked away into the darkness, lay the inhaler. It was as if Elizabeth knew!

A case was filed against Jack. The inhaler was sent off to forensics to examine fingerprints. But there were no prints to match the ones found on the inhaler! Edward was desperate to see Jack put behind bars, but he was clueless about how he could get Jack's fingerprints.

He suddenly remembered that during their college days, just to pass time, they had put their hand and footprints on posters with funny slogans on them, with their names signed below! Edward knew they were stored safely somewhere in their home because Elizabeth liked keeping all the mementoes of their life together. Sometimes being a hoarder has its benefits!

Finally, in one of the old trunks in the attic, he found the old posters! The posters were sent to the lab. Jack's fingerprints matched those on the inhaler! He was arrested, but still, it was not enough proof to put him behind bars.

That night, Elizabeth's spirit appeared and told Edward to look for a diamond bracelet which Jack had been wearing on his wrist that fateful day; it must have fallen somewhere in the garden. Maybe that would help? Surely that should be proof enough! Elizabeth helped him every step of the way. She knew he was heartbroken and perhaps bringing her murderer to justice would provide a balm to his aching heart even if it didn't bring his love back.

Edward searched for the bracelet in the lawn, combed the whole place and was ready to give up when he saw a shining thing near a bush. Now, no one could stop him from sending Jack to the gallows! He had also sent a summons to Jane, Jack's sister and Elizabeth's former best friend.

The bracelet was produced in court, and Edward asked Jane if she recognized the bracelet. She immediately revealed that it was gifted to Jack by their parents for their birthday. Jack kept denying everything, but after intensive cross-questioning and interrogation by the cops, he confessed that he had murdered Elizabeth to take revenge. The court sentenced him to death by hanging.

Edward was able to solve the case with the help of his beloved wife's spirit. That night, she appeared before them one last time to bid them a final goodbye and thank Edward. She was now at peace and told them that she would never return. Edward was heartbroken, but at peace knowing that *she* was at peace. He never married again.

He continued his work and spent more time bringing justice to those who had been wronged so that they wouldn't have to go through what he had gone through. And like a dutiful son-in-law, he looked after his old in-laws. Elizabeth's memories always stayed with them.

But some things are strange; Elizabeth did come every night! But only in her loving husband's dreams!

Theirs was an eternal love!

Immortal Love

In the mid-40s, there was a village in West Bengal named Chandanpur where Srinath Chaudhari and his beautiful, accomplished daughter, Manvi, lived. She was sixteen years old and Srinathji was middle-aged. He was known as Kaka in his village.

Kaka was a very respectable farmer with acres of land, several orchards and cowsheds. He loved helping his villagers financially, and to Manvi's despair, he never asked them to return anything they borrowed. Kaka was a handsome man with royal looks. He had lovely blue eyes and salt and pepper hair. On his forehead, he had a visibly big scar which he was born with. He often wondered about it.

Manvi was a little dusky like her mother with big brown eyes and long straight hair. She wanted to study, but due to the early demise of her mother, she could not as she had to look after her Baba, whom she loved dearly. Father and daughter had an amazing relationship.

Manvi was an excellent cook and homemaker. Whoever came home never left without having something to eat and a gift, which Manvi would make with her own hands; she always had many things ready, be it wooden accessories, paintings, embroidered sheets or even homemade knitted sweaters. The whole village sang her praises and she was loved by everyone.

Kaka was busy the whole day and only saw Manvi in the evenings. One day, while returning home from his farms, he saw some light in an abandoned hut, which was odd since no one lived there. Kaka thought to himself, "Who could it be? Someone is definitely there." He went across to the hut; the door was slightly open. He pushed the door open, and to his surprise, a white-haired swami sat there and smiled at him. The swami said, "Come in, Srinath." Kaka was totally astonished; he bowed down in respect, and with folded hands asked the swami why he had come to their village and how he knew his name.

The Swamiji smiled at him and said he had come all the way from Haridwar just to meet him, having heard much about Kaka's large-heartedness from his close disciples, especially Kaka's younger brother.

"I need your help. We're building a new temple for Kali Maa and an ashram, for which we need monetary help. Srinath, I know you won't disappoint me. I need about Rs five lakh from you."

On hearing this, Kaka's face dropped, and he was totally shocked. Swamiji saw this, and asked him, "Is there a problem?"

Kaka smiled and said, "I will try my best to help you. I will return to you in two days." Kaka came out of the hut very worried. The sun had set, and it was quite a cold evening.

Manvi was worried. What is taking Baba so long? He is never so late, she thought to herself. She set out to look for him and, on the way, she saw him approaching and heaved a sigh of relief. "What took you so long, Baba? Where were you? Baba, tell me why you look so worried? What happened?"

Kaka fondly smiled at her and said, "Nothing, *beti*, nothing to worry about."

Manvi was sure there was something troubling her father, but what could it be? While they ate a delicious dinner of fish curry and rice that night, Kaka told Manvi about the Swamiji and his request. Manvi was shocked and asked Kaka, "Where will you get so much money?"

Kaka assured her that he would get it from his younger brother who lived in the next village. He owed him money and Kaka would go to him the next morning.

The next day, Manvi packed some eatables and water for Kaka and said, "Take care Baba, and come home soon."

On his way to Janakpur, he stopped near a river to have a wash, eat, and rest. As he sat under a tree, a big black cobra bit him. He screamed in pain and ran towards the river but slipped on the rocky steps. His head hit one of the steps and he became unconscious. When he woke up, he was in the swami's hut and Manvi sat beside him.

Kaka looked normal, but he seemed to be in a trance. He said, "The same incident has happened before. A long time ago, I was a prince named Kartekeya and my kingdom consisted of 100 villages."

Manvi thought her beloved Baba had gone mad. These things did not happen, it was simply unbelievable. However, the Swamiji reassured Manvi that what her father had said was true because he had been a priest in his kingdom. Manvi was shocked. "How can this be, Swamiji?" Manvi asked.

The Swamiji said, "I have some parts of the Brighu (the book where every human being's past, present and future is written). Whether you believe in it or not, it is proof that this actually happened!"

Manvi could hardly believe her ears!

The Swamiji continued, "He was a very popular prince in his kingdom, and madly in love with his second cousin, princess Manorama, also called Manu. Incidentally, Kaka fondly called her Manvi! They lived in the same palace, but Manu's stepmother did not approve of the marriage because she wanted her nephew to get married to Manu. Kartekeya and Manu were childhood sweethearts."

Manvi got a little excited about the whole thing and was keen to know who the princess was. Was she alive or dead, she wondered? The Swamiji seemed to know everything, but when Manvi showered him with questions he was quiet and appeared to be in a fix, pondering the consequences were he to reveal the truth. Manvi kept pestering the Swamiji for days, but he was tongue-tied.

After a few days, Kaka was completely cured of the snakebite and fever. He remembered every detail of his past life and had the urge to know where Manu was. The Swamiji returned to Haridwar without taking the money. Nor did he disclose Manu's whereabouts.

Life went on for Kaka and Manvi as before. One day, Kaka returned home and saw Manvi shivering like a leaf. He touched her forehead, and at once he removed his hand; she was burning. In a short while the whole village was at Kaka's house. There was a sense of gloom as if their collective world was about to end. Every possible treatment was administered but alas, nothing seemed to work. Then, one day, in her semi-conscious state, Manvi called out, "Kartekeya O Kartekeya, please get those medicinal herbs from Chandi Hills. I will be cured at once and then we will get married."

Everyone was aghast. She was Kartekeya's Manu, the villagers thought. Kaka was in a state of shock and distress; Manvi lay unconscious, unaware of all this. Kaka, along with a few villagers, immediately left for Chandi Hills to get the herbs vital to save her life. When they reached the top of the hills, Kaka told the villagers that this was where a snake had bitten him, and he was pushed down into the gushing Ganges waters in his previous life. Princess Manu had suffered a dangerously high fever and her stepmother insisted he went to fetch the herbs that would cure her. It was a well-planned move by her. The scar on his forehead was because of that fall. It all made sense now.

They brought back the herbs and soon Manvi limped back to normalcy and remembered her past. The once happy home was now filled with darkness. Both father and daughter were in a fix with mixed emotions. Soon, a Panchayat was called to discuss this rather complicated problem this peaceful village had never faced.

After much discussion, Kaka said, "Let bygones be bygones. It is a miracle that this has happened. Our love had such a strong bond that if we were not fated to be together then, a twist of fate has brought us together in this life where we are completely content and happy."

Manvi fondly smiled at her Baba and fully agreed with whatever he said.

The Panchayat was dismissed. They happily continued their lives after making peace with the difficult hand life had dealt them.

After two years, Kaka got Manvi married to a rich, young zamindar who loved her dearly. Kaka led a quiet retired life and whenever Anando Chatopadhaya and Manvi came to visit, he was very happy. A year later, Manvi have birth to twins, a girl and a boy, whom Anando named Kartekeya and Manorama, unaware of the past. Manvi did not protest.

Anando was a very understanding and loving husband as well as a doting father. Soon, he started managing Kaka's affairs and they all lived together.

Later, the Swamiji told Manvi and Kaka that Satyen was the name of Manu's stepmother's nephew whom she wanted Manorama to marry; he was none other than Anando!

Well, this is destiny. Such is life and try as one might, nobody can fight it.

They too carried on with their lives and duties, grateful for whatever life had given them.

A Strange Bond

"Anuradha, wake up! It's almost noon! I don't understand why you study at night when you have all day to do so," Bhabhimaa yelled as she entered Anuradha's room bringing her morning cup of tea.

Anuradha was tall with a wheatish complexion. She had long thick hair and was quite social. She excelled in academics and was a computer science wizard. Her parents had died in a car accident. She was raised by her brother Vinay and her best friend and mother to her, her bhabhi (sister-in-law), Sugandhi. She was fourteen years younger than Vinay. She was in her third year of college.

Vinay was also tall, fair, and an extrovert. He was an electronics engineer. Sugandhi came from a very wealthy family. She and Vinay were childhood friends. She was beautiful, good-natured and religious. She loved Anu like her own child and did not have any children of her own. "Beta, are your friends coming to spend the Dussehra holidays with us?" asked Sugandhi.

"Oh! Bhabhimaa, why do you ask so many questions at this hour, my eyes are barely open!" cribbed Anuradha.

“Your dear Dadabhai (older brother) is waiting to have breakfast with you. You know he does not eat breakfast without you,” Sugandhi said.

“Hmm, as though you’ve eaten, why take Dadabhai’s name?” Anuradha teased.

“Okay, okay, meri maa, we both are starving, happy? Come on, get up or else I’ll splash cold water on you,” bhabhi threatened Anu.

Vinay was reading the paper when his baby sister came down.

“Good morning, Dadabhai!” said Anuradha, touching his feet.

“Oh! God bless you, beta, and may you get all the happiness. Anu do you know that the circus has come to town. Why don’t you take your friends to the circus? It will be fun. I can organize it. When are the girls coming?” he asked.

“In another two days, I suppose, Dadabhai?” Anu responded.

Anuradha and Sugandhi got busy making arrangements and doing up the house and bedrooms for the girls. They would be staying for at least a week. Sugandhi always looked forward to seeing Anu’s friends; she was very fond of them and vice versa.

The next few days saw Sugandhi cooking up a storm and freezing several specialties so that there would be more time spent with their guests and less time toiling in the kitchen! She loved having people over and so did Vinay. They hosted several parties and family get-togethers at their place.

Finally, the three girls arrived and the whole house was filled with laughter and chatter. Vinay and Sugandhi were excellent hosts to all their guests, but especially to Anu's friends. They gave her so much love and encouraged her in everything she did that she did not miss her parents.

Though Vinay did not always have the time, he tried his best to spend as much time as he could with the girls. He knew all of them since their childhood. They all called him 'Dadabhai,' were extremely fond of him, and respected him a great deal. The girls were thoroughly enjoying their stay at Janaki Kutir (Janaki was Anu's mother's name and her father's was Krishna).

Two days later, Dadabhai arranged for the passes for the circus, which was on the outskirts of their town, in a big maidan (open grounds). Sugandhi packed some sandwiches and poori-keema rolls for all of them. Anuradha and the girls were driven to the circus by her brother who told them he would also pick them up.

The circus had come to their town after a long time. They were all excited. It was well-lit with colourful shamianas (tents) and numerous well-decorated food stalls. It was a lovely evening, and the sun had almost set. The girls got good seats as they had special passes. The programme started on time. There were several performances. The first was the joker's act with the elephant, then came the chimpanzee on a scooter with a baby in a pram.

In the interval, they all enjoyed Sugandhi's goodies. As soon as the interval ended there was a trapeze show. They all sat at the edge of their seats! It was both terrifying and amazing at the same time! It was also exciting and beautiful. One by one, the artists performed their acts. Suddenly, the girls recognized the artiste who stood up and was ready to perform; he was Anu's old friend, Shekhar! They were all shocked to see him. They all knew he had a passion for performing and the circus, but they could never have dreamt that he would be here because he came from a wealthy family and it wasn't considered proper to join the circus. His mother had passed away when he was a child and his father had remarried. His stepmother Durga was very pretty but had a stern face. She was rather reserved and did not socialize much. The girls did not know anything else about her. Shekhar used to like Anuradha a lot when they were in school together. He was also a very bright and hardworking student.

The show was very enjoyable. They all rushed out to say hi to Shekar when it ended. Anuradha's friend Meera called out to him. "Shekhu! Shekhu!" He was stunned to see them and looked quite embarrassed to be seen here.

"Oh hello! How are you all? Nice to see all of you here." Shekhar faintly smiled at all of them. He did not look particularly pleased seeing this bunch here, especially Anu.

"What is all this Shekhar? How come you are here?" Anu worriedly asked her friend.

"Ah! I'll talk to you later, I'm in a bit of a rush, duty calls, please excuse me all of you, bye and take care." Shekhar left in a hurry. The girls did not approve of his behaviour at all.

Something seemed off. "Why did he behave so oddly?" grumbled the girls amongst themselves. Anuradha kept quiet. She knew there was something wrong, otherwise, he would never have behaved like this.

"Anu, what are you thinking about? Is your heart beating rapidly after seeing that stud?" Meera teased her friend.

"No, no, nothing of that sort. I was just wondering what his problem was? Why couldn't he speak to us?" Anu thought aloud.

As they exited the gates, Vinay waved out to them, and they all went home. That night, Anu could not sleep thinking of her friend, whom she loved dearly, but could never tell him this.

The next morning, she narrated the whole incident to her soul mate, Sugandhi. She was also quite shocked and upset upon hearing about all this. "Why don't you talk to his best friend, hmm, what's his name? Oh, I forget, *haan,* Anirudh!" Sugandhi suggested.

"I wonder where he is now? I've lost touch with all the guys. In fact, I saw Shekhar today after five years!" Anu told her *bhabhi*.

"Don't worry dear, we'll figure this out together," Sugandhi consoled her.

Soon the friends left, and once again, the college reopened for the final term. Everyone got busy with their studies and almost forgot about Shekhar. One day, after college, as Anuradha was returning home, she stopped by a shop to buy some groceries and saw someone approaching her. It was Shekhar. "Oh! Hello, Anu," he said, smiling at her.

"How are you? Where have you been? I haven't seen you for so many days," Anu said.

"There's a little café just round the corner. Can we go there and chat?" Shekhar asked.

They sat in the café that was tucked away from the busyness of the main road. They looked at each other; there was love in their eyes which spoke volumes.

"This is destiny," Anu told Shekhar. "I could have never imagined that I would ever see you again. We had lost touch," she said.

"Losing touch doesn't mean losing hope. I never lost hope, I knew one day we would meet never to be separated again because..." He hesitated. "I...well ...I LOVE you!" he blurted out, holding Anu's hand.

"Oh God!" she exclaimed. She could not believe that this day had finally come. She was finally hearing these words in real life rather than just in her dreams! She had tears of ecstasy in her eyes. Her only dream had come true. Shekhar did love her.

"I love you too but I never told you so because I was not sure about your feelings," she said.

Without letting go of her hands he said, "I was sure about your feelings and had full trust in my love and in you."

It seemed like the most perfect moment of all time. They were both lost in each other and very happy.

"Shekhar, why have you joined the circus?" Anu asked him.

"Ah! I knew this was coming," he sighed.

He narrated the whole story to Anuradha.

"I was in the ninth grade when the problems at home started. My mother started behaving oddly. She had never behaved like this before. I was totally ignored, my father had passed away that year, and she was the only one to look after me. But soon, her attitude sort of changed. I don't know what went wrong. Just before my birthday, she told me to leave the house. I was shocked. I did not know what to do. Where to go. She just told me this before I left: Survival of the fittest. That was all I had in terms of her blessings," he said sarcastically, but with a tinge of sadness.

"And I've survived. Not long after, I found out about this circus and joined the show. I went through rigorous training on the trapeze bars, and I'm now very successful. Strangely, my friend Anirudh has been extremely helpful. Every month he has been sending me money, and on my birthday, special gifts that I love. He is a true friend. He has even appointed this man who regularly visits me and asks about my well-being. He looks very fierce, but he's a nice chap. I've called Anirudh so many times to thank him and express my gratitude, but he brushes it off and is so humble. 'Oh, I'm not doing anything extraordinary,' he says. He is so sweet and modest. I'm really grateful."

Anuradha assured Shekhar that she would be by his side, come what may. She returned home that day and narrated the whole incident to Sugandhi, who was very happy for them but really perturbed by Shekhar's odd story. She shared the incident with Vinay and asked for his opinion.

As days passed by, Shekhar and Anu met regularly. Their love grew, but Anu was worried about Shekhar as he didn't look as happy as he used to be. The sadness reflected in his eyes. Anu wanted to help him but she didn't know how.

"Why don't you meet Anirudh? He may be of some help, giving us some direction," Sugandhi suggested to Anu.

"I don't know his whereabouts, and cannot ask Shekhar, because he'll wonder why I'm keen on meeting Anirudh," Anu explained.

One day, when she reached home, she heard unfamiliar voices coming from the house. She assumed that some relatives or friends had dropped in, as usual. As she entered, she saw a young man and an old lady seated in their living room, chatting with Vinay and Sugandhi.

"Come, Anu, meet our guests," Vinay called to his sister.

"Remember Anirudh?" he asked her, quite pleased.

"Shekhar's friend, Anirudh?" Anu asked in disbelief.

"Yes, you're right. I'm Anirudh, Shekhu's best friend," he said, smiling. "Good to see you after so long."

"Yes, it's been a while, hello!" Anu tried to smile at him and asked, "And this is your mother?"

Before Anirudh could say anything, Anu greeted her.

"Namaste, Aunty!"

"No, Anu, she's not Anirudh's mother," Sugandhi said, gently interrupting her.

It turned out, much to Anu's shock and surprise that she was Shekhar's mother, Mrs Durga Sen. Anu was speechless. She could not believe her eyes and ears. So many questions came to mind. Why was she here? What does she want? How does she know where we live? And most importantly, why had Anirudh come home with her? Was he part of this entire mother-son drama? If Shekhar found out about all this, the poor guy would be shattered.

"Anu," Durga interrupted her thoughts. "I've been living with this burden and so much guilt all these years. I had to play this dirty game with my Shekhu, whom I loved and still love, dearly. After his father's death, Shekhar's Mama (maternal uncle) threatened to kill his nephew and take all his wealth. I had sleepless nights, thinking about how to protect our son from that man. The only solution was to become villainous and degrade myself to save his life. All these years I've lived under immense pressure and pain, longing for my child. After I asked Shekhar to leave home, I contacted Anirudh and appointed a man through whom I sent money and gifts for Shekhar. This man is a bodyguard. I feared that my evil brother would do something terrible to my beloved son. Anirudh helped me a great deal by keeping this secret for so many years," she said, her eyes welling up with tears.

"Raghuvir, the bodyguard, told us about your relationship with Shekhar and has been following you. That's how I got your address, and I came here because with your help I can meet my dear son," Durga said.

On hearing the whole story Anu and Sugandhi were in tears; they had misunderstood her completely. They were not aware of the whole picture. "But where is the uncle now?" Anu asked Durga.

"He died a few weeks ago, and the dark clouds hanging above our lives, threatening to ruin everything, are now gone. That's why I rushed here as soon as I could. I couldn't bear to waste any more time," Durga told them.

"Anu, will you help me meet my son? Can you come with me?" Durga implored.

"We will all come with you," Vinay assured Durga.

They all went to the circus, and on reaching there, they were told that the trapeze artists were practising, so they were asked to wait for some time.

Durga was impatient. She was dying to see Shekhar. It was a wait of eight long years since she had seen him. She was worried that after all this, he would want nothing to do with her. It was a long wait. Suddenly, she saw a man coming out of the tent. She recognized that it was her son, Shekhar! He was shocked to see her and the others with her.

"Hello, Beta," she greeted him in a choked voice. She could not say anything else, as she broke down in tears. Anu narrated the whole incident to Shekhar who was stunned to hear that his mother had done all this to save him.

After hearing the whole story, he was in tears; he had hurt his mother, who was not at all the stone-hearted widow he thought his father's death had turned her into. She was but a mother in the truest sense of the word. It was a tearful reunion. They were all very happy.

As they say, all's well that ends well.

Is This Possible?

It was a full moon night; cold winds were blowing, and the sky was clear and starry. The household of zamindar Uttam Rai Chaudhuri anxiously awaited the arrival of the newborn, which Chaudhuriji and his wife Jonaki had yearned for ten long years.

Raiji, as he was fondly referred to by all, paced up and down the long corridors of his beautiful haveli, his anxiety was growing, and emotions running high! He was a rich zamindar, owner of 100 villages. He was a kind and helpful landlord, unlike many others, and loved by all. The couple had, year after year, held fasts, prayed at every temple, and made several pilgrimages, but all in vain!

It seemed that the Gods were finally pleased now, and a miracle was about to happen because so far, they had not been blessed. It was almost 2:00 a.m. and suddenly there was a new dawn! Raiji heard the first cry of the baby! Yes, it was surely a time to rejoice. The midwife came out and announced that Jonaki had given birth to a beautiful, healthy baby boy. Raiji, upon hearing the news, was overwhelmed and burst into tears. He immediately removed his golden bracelet and gave it to the midwife, for giving him this wonderful news, which he had waited for so long to hear.

The whole haveli was decorated, as though it was some big festival. The chants of the mantras, exuberant dances, the sound of shehnais and the enticing smells of a variety of sweets and delicacies for those who came to the haveli to have a first glimpse of the newborn, filled the air. He was indeed a gift from God; Raiji and Jonaki were finally blessed.

Jonaki belonged to a well-known business house, in Chittagong, West Bengal. She was cultured, talented, and extremely beautiful. She was married to Raiji who had a loving family. They were thrilled to be parents of a little wonder who had lovely thick hair, big black eyes, and a birthmark at a very unusual place, the spinal column.

The day of the naming ceremony came, and priests from all over the state came to bless the baby. The family priest, Maharishi Keshabanandaji, came all the way from the Himalayas to name and bless the baby. The baby was named Agastiya. But Maharishi was a little worried and told Raiji to take special care of the boy. He had a sense of impending doom, of something dark that was on the cards. He also noticed the birthmark but kept quiet. The ceremonies went off smoothly. The whole family was extremely thrilled with the baby's arrival. It was like a big and long festival. The child was extraordinarily brilliant.

Years passed by. Agastiya was home-schooled and spent much of his time being taught by his governess, Mrs Lisa. He shared a special bond with her and Raiji often commented about how close they were. Raiji teased Jonaki that Mrs Lisa was Agastiya's second mother. This annoyed Jonaki to no end.

At the age of nine, Agastiya was sent away from home to gain spiritual knowledge from Maharishi in his ashram after his thread ceremony, as was the tradition in their family. Raiji had also gone to the ashram at the age of nine after his thread ceremony. Away from home, in the ashram, Agastiya slowly started retreating into his shell. He missed his family but especially, Mrs Lisa.

Six months of his life at the ashram passed by. One morning, after his bath in the Holy Ganges, he passed out! When he regained consciousness, he had a high fever. Nobody could understand why this had happened. What could it be? Unfortunately, Maharishi was not in the ashram at that time. The hermits in the ashram were very worried. They asked Vaidji to come by and have a look. After a full check-up, he said it was typhoid.

Agastiya was semi-conscious, and his parents were called. He could not be moved from there, as he had a high fever and was at risk of getting some other infection. They all stayed in the ashram for close to a fortnight, till he was able to walk and take the long journey home.

He had become so weak; it took him a long time to recover. He had become so weak that he began to have frequent fainting spells which worried his family. After a few days, he returned to the ashram to finish the rest of his training. Within six months, his training in the ashram was successfully over and he returned home, and resumed tutelage under his beloved Mrs Lisa. He was a brilliant boy and a keen learner, whatever was taught to him he grasped quickly.

Two years passed by without any sickness or mishap. Mrs Lisa was away on leave, so Agastiya went to his paternal aunt's house as he enjoyed spending time there. He stayed there for ten days and then returned home.

One day, Jonaki noticed that Agastiya looked pale and had lost his appetite. Raiji told her not to worry and that he would be fine. Things did get better but he wasn't completely normal. One day, after Agastiya returned from the park, he went straight to his room and lay down but before Jonaki or anybody could ask him anything, the boy went into a coma! They were all shocked beyond belief. This young boy shouldn't have to face more blows in his life!

Raiji, Jonaki and the other members of the family decided that Vaidji should be summoned immediately. Unfortunately for the family, it would take him at least three days to get to them. Jonaki was inconsolable and highly disturbed as were Raiji and the rest of the family. They were all so helpless and worried sick. Agastiya was in a coma, but thankfully alive; he just lay still, unmoved, as though in deep slumber. The family tried waking the boy up, but everything proved futile. Three days seemed like three decades; it was an unending wait. Finally, the wait was over. Vaidji arrived along with other hermits who were experts in herbs and Ayurveda, and consoled the family; God-willing everything would be fine.

The examination went on for four long hours. They came out of the room where the family waited impatiently to hear what was wrong with their beloved boy and receive some solace, guidance, and a plan to heal him. To their shock, Vaidji said nothing was wrong; Agastiya was in a coma, and he could not do anything. Vaidji's medicines worked like magic on people but he too, for the first time, was helpless.

Raiji and Jonaki pleaded with Vaidji to cure their only son, promising him a fortune, but the latter was apologetic and said he couldn't possibly do anything. He reassured them to have faith in The Almighty and things would be fine. Unfortunately, for the family, especially for Agastiya's parents, it was an unending wait. The household was grief-stricken. Everyone could only think of one thing; whether Agastiya would survive and come out of this dreadful coma! But no one said anything, lest their darkest fear turned into reality! They were worried, confused and very sad. Jonaki and Mrs Lisa were inconsolable. Raiji, though a man of strong will, was broken from within. Seeing the state of the ladies and other members of the house, the patriarch of the family shed silent tears.

There was sorrow everywhere. As the news spread throughout all the villages, the villagers began to fast and pray. In temples, the priests started chanting mantras for the well-being of Agastiya. Every possible thing was done to bring him back to consciousness. But nothing seemed to work.

Three long months passed by. Finally, one morning, the wait was over, and a new dawn arose in everyone's life. As usual, after their bath and morning pooja, Raiji and Jonaki went to Agastiya's room, just to see him lying there, and to their astonishment, they found their son awake! He was sitting up in his bed smiling. Both parents hugged and kissed their little son, and their happiness knew no bounds. It was as though they themselves had come back to life from a deep, lifeless slumber.

Later, they asked him what happened, but he could not remember anything. He seemed very confused. The only thing he kept saying was he had some visions. What did he mean? It was very puzzling.

Three days later, his parents heard a loud scream from his room. It was almost midnight. They rushed to their child's room and saw him sitting up and panting. It was shocking to see him like this. Jonaki rushed towards him, held him tight, and consoled him. His father gave him water and tried to pacify him with his warm, comforting words. It took a while, but Agastiya calmed down. They asked why he had screamed to which he replied, "I had a bad dream!"

Someone was whipping him and pushing him into a cellar, he said, but he couldn't recall who or why. All he could say was that he felt very afraid. They sat beside their son and consoled him saying that it was just a bad dream, and it should be forgotten. That night, Jonaki slept beside her son, in his room.

The next morning, he woke up fresh and smiling, as though nothing had happened the night before. Mrs Lisa came early and together, they went through some schoolwork, which tired him out and he needed a nap again. While asleep, he saw strange visions again. This time, he saw a monastery and a big lawn. After he woke up, he told his parents about these visions and they were worried. What was their son going through?

Over the next few days, Agastiya had more frequent nightmares. What was so puzzling about these nightmares was that he felt they were real and not just bad dreams. This confused his poor bewildered and concerned parents even more. What did it really mean? He was able to describe them to a certain extent but he couldn't articulate how exactly they made him feel.

A few were recurring nightmares. One was of a dark-skinned girl, another of an army of soldiers. In yet another dream, he was in a dense forest full of wild animals like lions and jackals. He often woke up screaming at night and held his mother tight. The child and his family were going through traumatic times. He could not understand why he had such horrifying dreams. He began sleeping in his parents' room.

Raiji was very worried and could not bear to see their child in such a painful state anymore. He wanted his son to be his happy and bubbly self once again. He would give anything to bring normalcy back to his son's life. Members of his family wondered if his visit to his aunt's had something to do with his predicament. They suspected someone at his aunt's to have done some black magic on the boy and that's why he became comatose upon his return. This could also be the reason for his nightmares! Raiji tried to allay their fears, but people talked. It added to the stress of the distraught parents!

Soon, Durga pooja came and once again Maharishi came to their house and saw Agastiya who looked quite pale and sick with dark circles under his eyes due to so many sleepless nights. He was also very worried to see the child and his family in such a bad state. After the ceremonies, Maharishi took Raiji and Jonaki aside and suggested they take their son into the city to have a doctor examine him. "There is a time and place for our kind of treatment. This is not it. He needs modern medicine," Maharishi said.

Neither he nor Vaidji would be able to give him a proper diagnosis or medication to cure the ailment.

This seemed to be a very complicated case. They should leave immediately, he advised, taking their son to the city where a very close, old disciple of Maharishi lived. He would help find a specialist.

Raiji was happy with Maharishi's advice, but Jonaki was very sceptical about taking their son to the city for treatment. According to her, children could have bad dreams and screaming was just normal behaviour. But Raiji was convinced that this was something more than just bad dreams. They all took Maharishi's blessings and started preparing to go to the city, as soon as the festivities were finished.

Agastiya was unaware of their sudden plans to go to the city and the reason for the trip. Upon hearing the news, he was very excited and jumped around the house teasing his cousins that they were going to be left behind; only he was going with his parents and was going to have a rollicking time. The other children in turn whined to their parents; why was he going to the city while they had to stay back and study?

Agastiya implored his mother to let him take a caseload of toys and allow his darling pet dog, Chief, to accompany them. But his mother firmly put her foot down. He could take a few toys and books but the dog was definitely not going with them. He sulked the rest of the day, but his mother was unmoved. To cheer him up, his father bought him some hot jalebis and samosas and the innocent child was happy once again.

The next morning was the day of departure. The family was anxious about what lay ahead. They all looked sad but pretended to be happy in front of the little child who jumped with joy and thought this was all just a fun mini vacation. He took the blessings of all the elders in the family and hugged all his cousins. They all wished him good luck.

It was an overnight train journey to reach Calcutta. They arrived early the next morning. Raiji left the coach to look for Maharishi's disciple. He had only a description to go by and didn't know who this Shishir babu was. Suddenly, he saw a familiar face walking towards him, and to his surprise, the disciple was none other than his childhood friend Shishir! What a happy coincidence! It was lovely to see each other after so many years. They had studied together in Chittagong when they were kids and were the best of friends. Raiji admitted to Shishir that he was relieved that he was not going to stay with a stranger, but a childhood friend and guru-bhai.

On reaching Shishir's house, and freshening up, Raiji explained the situation to his friend and his wife Suhagi. They too were quite shocked at hearing what the little child was going through. Suhagi, a kind-hearted lady, was in tears. Shishir assured Raiji and Jonaki that they would help in any way possible. Shishir said that he knew one of the city's best psychiatrists and would fix an appointment with him. Agastiya's parents saw a ray of hope. That night, all of them including Agastiya, slept well.

The next morning, Shishir called Dr Ghosh, and to their disappointment, his secretary informed them that the doctor was out of town and would only return in a week's time. For Raiji and Jonaki, their life came to a standstill. They had hoped that Agastiya would get some help as soon as they arrived but that's not how life works. They were impatient but could do nothing but wait.

Shishir and Suhagi, who had no children of their own, wanted to show Agastiya their beloved City of Joy and some of its favourite tourist spots. For the next few days, they explored the innards of Calcutta. They visited the glorious Howrah Bridge (now known as Rabindra Setu), which was once the third-longest cantilever bridge in the world! They admired the magnificent gates of the Kalighat Kalibari and the uniquely made statue of the Goddess Kali. Agastiya was shown the famous Hooghly River and rode on the tram, a Calcutta landmark. He was fed copious amounts of *puchkas,* as they had some time on hand and he had come to the big city for the first time.

They also arranged a picnic at the Botanical Gardens in Shibpur. Perhaps a day spent amidst hundred-year-old trees would soothe the fraying nerves of Raiji and his family? Shishir babu and his wife went above and beyond and made the trip memorable, so much so that for a little while Raiji and Jonaki had forgotten about all their troubles and the real reason for their visit. They laughed, ate and made merry and the day was filled with fun and joy. Shishir and Raiji went on a nostalgic trip, talking about their childhood and youth. The ladies got to know each other and enjoyed young Agastiya's company.

The week flew by. Their sightseeing was coming to an end. As they returned from the picnic, they saw some men working on one of the roads. They were quite tanned and muscular from the long hours of labour, toiling in the sun. Agastiya noticed them and started yelling incoherently, trying to hide behind his bewildered mother. Everyone was stunned by the sudden change in his behaviour. Raiji explained to him that there was nothing to fear and that they were just workers, repairing the road. Agastiya soon forgot about the incident, but the others were left worried.

Finally, the wait was over; the day came when they would finally meet Dr Ghosh and perhaps get an explanation. Agastiya and his parents were accompanied by Shishir to see the doctor. At the doctor's clinic, they waited for about fifteen minutes before they were called inside. Raiji pleaded with Dr Ghosh to do something quickly because they could not see their child in pain anymore.

Dr Ghosh was very pleasant, understanding and considerate too. He was a close friend of Shishir's and reassured them, asking them to wait outside while he spoke to Agastiya. Jonaki insisted that she wanted to be with her son, as he would get scared to be alone with a stranger.

After his initial examination and questioning, Dr Ghosh told them, "As a friend, I'd like to tell you that this isn't just bad dreams. There could be another possibility. I'm a medical professional and would normally have prescribed some medicines to help him relax because nightmares are usually a result of stress, but my instinct tells me there is more to this. You may have read about such things but never seen them."

This confused Raiji and Jonaki. Perhaps it was the stress of the recent events or perhaps it was her lack of schooling, but Jonaki suddenly became rather defensive. "He's just like the other children. This happens a lot in our village. It's not out of the ordinary," she tried to helplessly defend her son.

Raiji looked uneasy.

"Yes, of course he is just like the other kids," Dr Ghosh comforted Jonaki. "But what he's going through right now, these visions, may not be your everyday childhood nightmares."

"You should see a specialist," he told Raiji who seemed to be the more reasonable one right now. "Someone who has more experience in this field. It is very possible that he's remembering his past."

Raiji and Jonaki stared at him in shock and disbelief. They could not digest what the doctor had told them. Jonaki insisted that their son wasn't mad! Raiji apologized to the doctor for her behaviour as she was really stressed.

"Modern medicine is sceptical about the presence and occurrence of such things. I, too, have only heard of and never actually treated someone like this in my practice. But my gut says that this is the most likely explanation for Agastiya's visions," explained Dr Ghosh.

Raiji and Jonaki looked even more confused so Dr Ghosh continued. "This could be a case of reincarnation, and a psychotherapist who is well-versed in Past Life Regression (PLR), therapy can help Agastiya and you find answers. I have a friend who has done extensive work in this field, and I'm sure he will be able to help. Give me a few minutes," he said, and left the room.

He returned after what seemed like an eternity. "Dr Ashish Sen will see Agastiya and you tomorrow," he smiled. Dr Ghosh had asked for a personal favour from Calcutta's best psychotherapist so he would see Agastiya as soon as possible.

The next morning, they all went to see Dr Sen, accompanied by Dr Ghosh. Dr Sen explained that the best way to know if the visions were indeed more than just nightmares was through a session of hypnosis and if they were willing, he had set aside time that day itself, for a session!

"Most people think of magicians as evil, casting a spell on others to get all their dirty secrets and loot them. Hypnotherapy is far from that. Imagine a relaxing sleep where you can speak and explore your dreams. You can learn so much about yourself that you didn't know before? That's how hypnotherapy helps my patients. And I hope it'll help young Agastiya too," he said, smiling.

This put Raiji and Jonaki at ease, although they still couldn't quite wrap their head around all this information! Dr Sen explained that he would start with some relaxation techniques with Agastiya to make him comfortable so it would be easier for him to go into a state of hypnosis. If a patient was tense, it could create blockages in tapping into the subconscious, he explained.

"You may remain here or if he's okay with it, wait outside while I chat with Agastiya. Are you okay with that *beta*?" Dr Sen was a kindly man with a warm smile that could put anyone at ease.

Agastiya nodded.

"Don't worry. You can come in any time if he's uneasy. We don't use force here. This process only works with the full cooperation of the patients."

Dr Sen shut the door. He began by talking to Agastiya about his favourite subject - his pet dog, Chief. Of course, Agastiya needed just one prompt and he went on to wax eloquent about the hilarious antics of his beloved four-legged friend. Raiji and Jonaki could hear giggles and little chirps of excitement from inside. Agastiya was generally a happy and curious child and followed Dr Sen's prompts to relax into a deep hypnotic trance.

Dr Sen asked him a series of questions. The wheel had started moving! Finally, Agastiya started pouring his heart out. He could remember his previous births! Within the first ninety minutes itself, several stories emerged. He recollected being a slave in Africa and being traded. His name in that birth was Gome. He was poverty-stricken, with no food and scanty clothing. He was treated mercilessly by his master, who whipped him and put him in the cellar for days as punishment for not completing his work properly on time.

Once, he was so tired that he had to lie down but was punished with a red-hot iron rod on his back. Incidentally, he had a birthmark in the same spot in his current birth as well! He screamed in agony but was forced to carry heavy sacks even though he could barely stand. The only ray of hope in his depressing life was Jane, a slave girl in his master's house. Gome was attracted to her and she liked him too. But unfortunately, they never got to meet each other, because of their inhuman master. On one occasion, they were lucky enough to meet and Gome promised Jane that he would marry her.

One day, when Gome was cleaning his master's room, he saw something shining. It looked like gold to him; to his surprise it was a sack of gold coins. His hands shivered, as he could not believe what he saw. He had never seen so much money in his entire life. Greed raised its ugly head and he stole the sack and ran away that night. With the stolen gold he was able to become wealthy like a king overnight and betrayed his first love, marrying a rich girl. When Jane learned about this, she was shattered and cursed that he would never be happy.

Agastiya seemed to be disturbed but keen to go on. It was as if he was a fish seeking deeper waters. He spoke of a monastery. He was a bhikshu in Montana, USA, a Buddhist monk, and his name was Buddhananda. The monastery was not far from Arlee. He had a very depressing childhood, as he was the eleventh child of his parents. He did not get the love and care that he desired. He was made to do all sorts of odd jobs at an age when children are meant to be carefree and play. He was made to slog. Even though he wanted to be like other children who went to school, played and ate to their heart's content, his parents were not well-to-do and had so many mouths to feed. One day, some monks were passing by and that was when he decided to run away from home and lead a monastic life.

Dr Sen paused the session. Agastiya awoke and looked around. He looked rested but tired. The doctor decided to stop for the day and asked if Raiji would like to continue.

"Dr Ghosh had a hunch but my session with Agastiya confirms that he is indeed remembering his past lives. It is very rare that we see something like this. Usually, most traumas, fears or phobias are addressed by hypnosis; a trip into the deep subconscious when a patient can identify exactly what's bothering them. But in your son's case, we are travelling back several births and exploring lifetimes. It must be exhausting for him but he's doing great. I have the notes from today's session that you can take home and review. I urge you to continue if you really want some sort of resolution to these recurring nightmares or as you call them, visions," the doctor said.

"Of course. We will be back. We are so grateful to you," Raiji said, tears in his eyes.

They returned two days later and then again, three days after that. Agastiya seemed to be responding rather well to these sessions and spoke about being a girl in London, though he could not remember the girl's name as she was a barmaid and was addressed as 'Miss'. He could not remember anything else about his birth as a girl. He also told Dr Sen that he was born to a young couple, but only survived for two days.

Raiji and Jonaki sat motionless after hearing the recordings on the Dictaphone. They had seen Dr Sens's notes as well and couldn't fathom how their little child was able to somehow recollect details of his past lives. Some of it was so traumatic! They didn't know what to say or do! Their child, still their baby, seemed to even have a different voice as he talked about these people, these versions of himself! It disturbed the poor parents. They prayed for this to somehow be over soon. But the sessions continued, and during the next few sessions and a few weeks later, new facts emerged.

Agastiya, in his hypnotized state, also recollected that he saw jungles and wild animals and a man, perhaps a hunter, killing them mercilessly. He also told the doctors that he was an artisan, and his name was Kanu. He was in a huge warehouse, where he carved things on wood. He could not remember more of his life as an artisan.

After many sessions, things became clearer. Strangely, whatever Agastiya had told Dr Sen, the one common theme seemed to be trauma and immense unhappiness in his past lives. All that could have built up, causing his recurring nightmares and visions. Dr Sen told Agastiya's parents that sometimes it is essential to visit traumas in our past to help with our present.

It was simply out of a movie! So many births and lifetimes! So much had this little soul endured and was being haunted by. It was indeed beyond anyone's imagination.

Dr Sen agreed that this was a very rare case and though he had come across people who had regressed into their past lives, he had never come across any such patient in his medical career spanning forty years! "But I assure you, a few more sessions will definitely help rid him of these nightmares, these visions as you call them, alongside regular relaxation and self-hypnosis techniques," he said confidently.

A few months passed by, and at last, the treatment was over and extremely successful. Agastiya was cured. He had forgotten everything and had not had any unpleasant dreams or terrifying nightmares. He impatiently waited to go back home to his cousins and friends and of course, his best friend, Chief.

Dr Sen and Dr Ghosh told Raiji that this was an unforgettable experience and experiment and a professional victory in the field of PLR and psychotherapy. They had also achieved and learned something from this rare case, acknowledging that nothing is impossible in this world.

Dr Sen told Raiji and Jonaki that it could take some time for Agastiya to lead a completely normal life. It wasn't taboo to talk about these past lives, but one must remember that these things happened in the past, and while they can be a useful tool, it is important to focus on the present.

"There's medicine and therapy but there's nothing greater than the love and care that you provide him," said Dr Sen, as they were about to leave.

"Good luck, Agastiya, you have been wonderful," said Dr Ghosh.

Agastiya touched their feet and took their blessings.

In the past few months, they had all become extremely fond of him, as he was an adorable kid. They both wished Raiji and his family a happy and peaceful life ahead. The couple gave each doctor a token of their immense gratitude: An idol of Goddess Durga.

Both doctors were overwhelmed upon receiving this token of love and gratitude. Agastiya's parents were after all indebted to them for life.

They also thanked Shishir and Suhagi who were both in tears, on seeing little Agastiya jumping happily as he was ready to go home. Raiji and Jonaki thanked them for their hospitality and patience in bearing with them for so many months and finally began their return journey home.

On reaching home they got a very warm welcome. The whole house was decorated with lights and marigolds. Maharishiji came to meet the family and bless them. He confided to Raiji that he knew Agastiya's state but wanted them to get better and more modern treatment by specialists and not Vaidji. They were indebted to the Rishi.

And all was well once again in their small world.

The Mystery of the Knitted Sweater

Summer was approaching, but exam fever was still on. There was high tension in the Apte household as the exams were tough. There were six children altogether, four boys and two girls. They were the children of two brothers, and they all lived together in a mansion in Delhi. The older brother had four sons: Anand, Abhay, Karan and Sahil. The younger brother had twin daughters, Anjari and Manjari. They all went to the same school.

The boys were extremely fond of the twins and were very protective of them too. Anand and Abhay were much older than their brothers and cousins. The fathers, Ram and Laxman, were in the furniture business and were often on tours for business purposes. Their wives, Rajeshwari and Sukanya, had their own small businesses offering cooking classes. It was a close-knit family where both mothers instilled strong family values in the children.

The same rules applied to all six children. And punishments too! Rajeshwari was Badi Maa and Sukanya was Maa. They both came from big business families and were talented, courteous, and amicable towards each other.

The children looked forward to their holidays because they were going to visit their grandparents after a very long time. They were going all the way to Patnitop, a lovely hill station in Jammu and Kashmir.

Their grandfather, Mr Atmaram Apte, was a staunch Gandhian and had fought in the freedom struggle. He had worked with Gandhiji and other well-known freedom fighters of his time and had been to jail several times during the struggle for Independence. His wife Lata Apte was also a freedom fighter. That's how they met, fell in love and got married. Daduji, as he was known to all, had started the furniture business, which his sons ran while he chose to retire in the hills. He had bought a beautiful house that was made of pure teak wood. A stream flowed behind the house which was surrounded by lovely pine trees and lush green lawns. It was a picturesque view. The children had only seen the pictures of the house but now they would be going to stay there.

Daduji, Ammaji and his stepsister, Gayatri, who was a widow, lived in the huge palatial house. This was the first time that the children were going to visit and were extremely excited and looked forward to the trip as it had been long since they had met their grandparents. They were not at all fond of Gayatri, or Phui as they called her, since she disapproved of their constant playing and pranks. She was generally irritable, nagging and very conservative. But their respective mothers always taught them to give due respect to their elders, and not to misbehave or be discourteous.

The exams were soon done with, but there were still ten days to leave. Orders for new woollen sweaters were placed with the family knitter and measurements for new clothes were given to the tailor, as it would be colder than what the children were accustomed to in Delhi.

The excitement mounted, and all kinds of plans were made. Anand, being the eldest, was the leader, and the rest followed him blindly. They were all partners in crime, in whatever they did. It was a gang, and no outsider was allowed in on their pranks or secrets. Everyone in school was envious of the cousins.

Soon, it was the day to pack and the whole household was full of excitement and commotion. Rajeshwari assigned the two boys Karan and Sahil to fetch the clothes and sweaters respectively so that they could save time and do other things as well. Karan went to pick up the clothes and Sahil went to the knitter. The knitter, Asim Bhai, was not there and so his helper handed over the heap of sweaters to Sahil and he returned home with them.

Eventually, all the essentials had been crammed into trunks and bags and the day of departure had finally arrived. Lots of snacks were packed for the long train journey. The children had also stuffed games, books, packs of cards and other treasures in their canvas backpacks. Manjari had packed her embroidery kit, as she wanted to learn some new stitches from her grandmother, who was an expert. The train journey was long and beautiful, and they were all in vacation mood, totally relaxed and happy.

Rajeshwari's brother, who used to visit Daduji quite often, much to her disapproval, was also coming to meet his sister and her family. All the children were extremely fond of their Mani Mama (Mansukh Lal Khare). Rajeshwari's parents did not approve of him, as he did no work, except play the fool and wander about everywhere. Rajeshwari did not welcome him in their house, but Daduji and Ammaji were very fond of him, even though Daduji was quite the disciplinarian and a tough nut to crack.

But Mani would surprisingly get away with everything. He was not married. According to his parents, no parent would risk giving their girl to a good-for-nothing man. He was considered the black sheep of the family.

The kids looked forward to seeing him at the station with Daduji. The train slowly crawled into the station, and the kids excitedly peeped out of the window, to have a glimpse of their dear Daduji and Mama. As the train halted, they saw Daduji standing right in front of their coach. They all yelled in excitement, while their parents tried to shush them, as they were all embarrassed by all the noise, but in vain.

They all embraced Daduji, almost making him trip. Their happiness knew no bounds. As they all greeted Daduji, they saw a clownish man walking gleefully towards them with his mouth full, chewing paan. He was Mani Mama with his clumsy gait and shabby appearance. Despite his dishevelled looks, the kids were obsessed with him. He was always on their side and bought them a lot of goodies. They all hugged Mama, but Rajeshwari, in dismay, ignored her elder brother and did not give him much attention.

It was good to see Daduji ramrod straight as ever, looking fit as a fiddle. They all headed for home, which was a good thirty-minute drive from the station. The whole Apte family was happy to be together again. It was a beautiful drive home, very scenic with majestic mountains, deep valleys and greenery everywhere, the perfect weather for a vacation. A welcome respite from the unbearable Delhi heat.

As they neared the house, Daduji showed them the Naag temple road, which they insisted on calling Mall Road because it reminded them of the Mall Road in Shimla! This little hill station was no Shimla, but it was a cute hamlet in the hills. The road had a handful of businesses and a Naag temple and was barely five minutes away from their house. There was also a small library, a pet shop, a bakery and a curio shop.

The children's excitement grew, as they knew they were going to have a blast. As they neared the house, they saw an artistic signboard on which was inscribed their house number; it looked beautiful. Daduji explained he had specially got the board made, asking for this particular number. They entered the house gates and there stood another favourite person of theirs: Ammaji, their grandmother, an ever-smiling, frail old lady, the backbone of the family. She greeted all of them with great warmth and open arms. One person missing from this family reunion was Gayatri Phui, who was as usual in her room, probably sulking at the prospect of her peace being destroyed!

Ammaji explained laughing that she had had some disagreement with Daduji, her brother, and had since retired to her room! The two often argued and fought like small children.

Daduji showed them around and they were all thrilled to see the palatial house. It was beautiful and much larger than what they had expected. They loved the many corridors and little rooms and storage *kothris*.

Soon everyone got settled into holiday mode with the mothers busily chatting with Ammaji, the fathers relaxing with Daduji and exchanging notes about the business and the kids exploring the house and surrounding areas with Mani who was extremely comfortable with kids. He spent most of his time with them.

Around lunchtime, the family finally got to meet Phui. As usual, she had a frown on her face, and looked disapprovingly at the daughters-in-law, and dotingly at her nephews, who were her favourites. She always nagged Anjari and Manjari for no apparent reason and Mani Mama too, who, despite bringing sweets and gifts for everyone, was always in her bad books.

Gayatri Phui was Daduji's only sister. Her husband had died at a very young age and had left her a fortune. She was childless and not welcome by her own in-laws, so Daduji invited her to live with them. She was extremely fond of Ammaji since she was perhaps the only one who tolerated all her tantrums. Despite being so wealthy and financially secure, she was a miser and never spent a penny on anyone. Instead, she would ask Daduji for money for her needs. She was very fond of good food and going out. Her room was always locked, and only got cleaned in her presence. She never let anyone come into her room or even peep in. This was how it was ever since she came here. Everyone just accepted her the way she was – a strange person.

As the evening approached, there was a chill in the air, and the children started feeling cold, so Rajeshwari and Sukanya unpacked their things. As Rajeshwari unpacked the clothes from the heavy trunk, she noticed some sweaters which they hadn't ordered! She called Sahil and asked him if he knew about the sweaters. He, too, was surprised. He explained to Rajeshwari that since Asim Bhai was not there, his servant had simply handed him a pile of sweaters and hats and must have mistakenly given them someone else's clothes too! The sweaters were all the same shade of green, with a motif embroidered on them, in a strange script they didn't understand.

Sahil told Anand about the mistake, and he too was surprised since this had never happened before. Anand mentioned this at the dinner table when everyone had arrived. Mani Mama wasn't feeling well so he was upstairs resting. Daduji told them not to worry, such mistakes happen, and when they returned to Delhi, they should return the sweaters to Asim Bhai and inform him about the shop's mistake.

That night, they all slept early, as they were all very tired after the long train journey. It was a chilly night, but the next morning was bright, and not at all cold. They all decided to explore the little town and the surrounding areas. The elders decided to just visit the temples close by.

The kids and Mani Mama, who was now feeling better, wanted to explore the town, which was awesome. They also casually mentioned to Mani Mama about the sweaters, and he too was surprised, but they soon forgot all about them in their keenness to explore. The whole day went by with a lot of fun and frolic. The kids did a lot of sightseeing, ate some local delicacies and by evening, returned home where Ammaji was waiting with hot ginger tea and lovely cheese rolls, which they all loved.

As the evening grew, they all started feeling cold, so Anand went up to his room to get his sweater. To his shock, the green sweaters that didn't belong to them were missing! He was shocked; who could have taken them, and why? He told everyone about the missing sweaters, and the whole house was searched, and the servants questioned, but no one knew anything about them. They were all a little perturbed, but Daduji told them not to worry; they were probably misplaced. The children looked dubiously at each other, wondering how that was even possible! Mani Mama asked if Daduji's friend, who was in the police force, could do something, but Daduji said that the police usually never wasted their time on trivial matters; they had much bigger fish to fry! He was quite bothered by this, as something like this had never happened before in their peaceful life, and that too just as his dear grandchildren had come from so far to visit!

A few days passed by, but unfortunately, no missing sweaters turned up. Soon, the children forgot about the incident and so did the others and they enjoyed being pampered by the grandparents. Manjari took a keen interest in learning embroidery from Ammaji, and the matriarch was more than happy to teach her the art.

One day, Mani Mama had to leave very suddenly without any reason for this sudden departure. The family started teasing him asking if he had a girlfriend who had summoned him at once! Daduji teased Rajeshwari that soon she would have a sister-in-law to fuss over, but as always, Rajeshwari did not seem pleased with her brother's randomness.

Mani told everyone that he had a group of friends who had invited him and that he would be away for a week. The elders wondered if he had got into bad company, indulging in gambling and alcohol, but he had never discussed anything with his sister or brother-in-law, Ram. He bid everyone goodbye and left. The children were upset because all the fun was gone with him.

The remaining days passed by uneventfully for the Apte family.

Reading, board games, endless rounds of rummy and delicious food combined with the fresh mountain air made for a fabulous time. They all had a great time with the grandparents amidst brief appearances of the grumbling Phui, who yearned for them to leave, as she did not like noise; the house echoed with the loud cackles of excited children.

One day, while exploring the little shops along Naag temple road, as they came out of the small grocery store, Anand spotted a scary-looking man wearing the very same sweater that had gone missing! He couldn't believe his eyes! The man exited the Naag temple and looked around shiftily. Anand was shocked and stood there motionless. Before he could tell his cousins, the man had vanished into thin air. His siblings were surprised to see their elder brother in a trance-like state. They asked him repeatedly why he looked like he had seen a ghost?

"We need to go back home," he whispered urgently. "It isn't safe here."

The others were alarmed by the urgency in his voice but followed his instructions and they hurried home. He shut the door to their room and then told the children what he had seen. They were all shocked! There was unending silence. They all racked their brains trying to come up with a solution.

"We should keep an eye on the temple, maybe hang around those quaint shops to see if we spot the man again," Anand suggested.

"I think we should tell the grown-ups," Abhay suggested. "Daduji knows the locals and this small town. We are just visitors, what can we do?"

The others didn't think the elders would do much. They'd probably just shush them, brushing it away as a figment of their imagination.

"Let's be on the lookout for anything suspicious but let's keep this to ourselves for now, until we know more," Abhay said.

They agreed to make this their secret mission for the next few days. It was difficult to keep it from the adults because they really thought this was serious and perhaps, they were too young to handle it alone.

A week passed and Mani returned. The children were happy and relieved to see him, as they thought he would lend them a patient ear as he always did. They all told him about the sweaters and the gruff-looking man near the Naag temple, but to their dismay, he told them to think nothing of it and laughed it off. The children felt rather helpless but did not tell the rest of the family knowing that if Mani didn't take them seriously, the other elders would not.

That night, as they sat in their room, trying to focus on the game of cards instead of worrying about the sweaters, they heard a loud hammering coming from what seemed to be the next room!

"Probably one of the helpers fixing something," Abhay said.

Curious as they were, they went next door. But it was empty. Their parents were still out on their walk and there was no one in the room! The hammering continued. They investigated the other rooms but there was no sign of anyone or anything. Quite alarmed, the children wondered if they should tell Phui. A light seemed to be on in her room, but they feared her sharp tongue and bitter nature. She was bitter about everything and always complained that Daduji was the favourite of her parents because he was a boy; her father had never pampered her. She was jealous of her brother. Bitterness had sprouted in her since childhood, even though Daduji took excellent care of her. The kids plucked up the courage and went to her room and knocked, but there was no reply.

"Could she be asleep already?" wondered Manjari.

"Maybe she's dead," Anjari looked hopeful.

"Shush! Don't say that. She may be mean but she's still our family," reprimanded Abhay.

"She probably fell asleep before turning off the light," concluded Anand.

The hammering had now stopped, and the kids reluctantly went back to their room and packed up the cards because all interest in winning a round of rummy had vanished!

The next morning, they told Mani what they'd heard the night before even though he had pooh-poohed their earlier story.

"Oh, you children have such fertile imaginations. Sound travels far in these hills. I mean, you can hear Ramdas' goat bells in the morning if you wake up at a decent time you know!" He winked at them in amusement.

After a sumptuous breakfast, they went for a walk around Mall Road. Thankfully, they didn't see Phui in the morning and were quite relieved. They really didn't enjoy any interaction with her! The girls wanted to buy earrings and other knick-knacks from the small store next to the Naag temple even though the boys usually disapproved. But when Mani Mama was around, he'd indulge the kids no matter what. He bought the girls anything and everything they wanted.

While waiting with the boys and watching the townsfolk go about their daily activities, Anand suddenly froze in shock and stared! The others followed his gaze and to their horror and surprise found themselves looking at Phui in the market speaking to a man who had one of the same green missing sweaters on! They tried to strain their ears to catch what Phui was saying but she was at a distance.

"See, I told you she's evil," said Anjari. "You didn't believe me," she taunted.

The children wondered if there was any truth to Anjari's words. Was this bitter old lady an evil villain? Was she involved in something sinister? He was the same man whom Anand had seen two days ago wearing the same sweater.

"There's no doubt. It's the same man I saw. He has that annoying look even when he isn't frowning," Anand said.

They were still figuring out what to do next when the girls and Mani Mama returned, but the man had gone and thankfully Phui too had not seen them. The boys told Mani Mama what had just happened. He took it all in and said, "Okay. Maybe there is something to your tales. Don't say a word at home. I'll take care of things," he assured them.

They nodded, still stunned by this new development.

That night, at the dining table, they were all exceptionally quiet and the elders wondered what could have happened to quieten this rambunctious bunch. But as always, they did not pry, assuming it was some teen tiff they would get over the next day! However, Ammaji did not like silence, and she asked Manjari if she and her sister had had a fight with the boys, and she assured her that all was fine, and they were just tired and would go to bed early. Ammaji was satisfied with the reply. All the children went to bed early but hoped Mani Mama would have some news for them. They didn't hear from him and fell asleep reluctantly.

At around 4:00 a.m., Abhay woke up with a start. He could hear hammers pounding somewhere close by and he just sat up and wondered if he was imagining it or if he was really hearing those sounds! As he continued to hear them, he woke everybody up, and they too heard the sounds which were surprisingly coming from their own house, but from where? They had already searched the whole house the previous day!

They woke up Mani Mama who generally slept like a log. He was surprised to see the bewildered young gang standing beside his bed. When he asked them what the matter was, they told him the reason, and he too was stunned. Together with Mani Mama they combed the whole house, lawns, backyard, and outhouses, but could not find anything. They could still hear the hammering sounds loud and clear. The sun was about to rise, so Mani Mama suggested that they return to their rooms before Daduji or anyone else got up and saw them. They would do something in the morning. They all returned to their rooms as they trusted Mani Mama completely and expected him to do something in the morning, even though the rest of the family didn't think much of him.

The children got up later than usual the next morning having slept so late the night before! They were scared and worried because they could not digest the fact that Phui may be involved in anything dubious, even though no one quite liked her. But what they had seen was true: She was speaking to a stranger who was wearing one of the missing sweaters. There were strange sounds they couldn't trace the origin of! The kids had several questions but no answers.

As they got up and went for breakfast, the fathers told them that Daduji and Ammaji had organized a picnic for them, and they would be leaving shortly. Just what the kids and Mani did not want at that moment, as they were planning to keep an eye on Phui and her movements. They wanted to be home that day but could not refuse their grandparents and disappoint them.

"Let's pretend that everything is normal so no one suspects anything," Mani Mama cautioned the kids.

Excited to be part of a plan which a grown-up was in on but also nervous, they packed their things and headed for the picnic spot.

English Point was a popular picnic spot not too far from home. They put on a brave and cheerful front and tried to enjoy the games, running around and exploring the place with the family. It was beautiful, with lush green lawns, beyond which were rolling plains surrounded by mountains and cascading waterfalls. Everyone was happy and Mani had the kids in splits with his silly pranks.

As was the norm regarding family picnics, there was enough food to feed an army! After lunch, all the seniors decided to take a catnap, but the kids and Mani wanted to explore the whole area. The adults were confident that Mani would take good care of the children. The gang walked quite a bit and soon they came to a stream and wandered about looking for the end of the stream. They walked along the stream and suddenly saw eight men coming out of an opening. To their shock, they were all wearing the missing green sweaters with a sort of strange code knitted on them!

They tried to hide out of sight behind the bushes from where they saw the men carrying big wooden cases crossing the stream and heading towards the border. The girls trembled with fear and hid behind Mani Mama holding him tight, and the boys, though they put up a brave front, were also very scared. Now they were sure that something was very wrong as they could make out that these were not the good guys.

They waited till they saw the men cross the stream. Mani Mama suggested that he would go into the tunnel and have a look along with Anand while the rest of them waited outside. However, they all opposed him as they did not want to wait outside alone. Mani Mama didn't want to leave the girls outside but couldn't take them back either as there would be a thousand questions! So, it was decided that they would all go inside the tunnel and deal with it together, come what may! They took deep breaths and headed inside the tunnel, quite scared. It was a long tunnel, and it seemed to be never-ending as they kept walking and walking. It was exhausting but they rallied on!

Finally, they reached an area where the tunnel seemed to widen and here, they found several crates stacked and a messy pile of the green sweaters. Mani went closer to inspect them and announced that there were bombs and ammunition in the crates!

"This is definitely not legal or safe! This is probably a hideout, and they use this space as a base to supply arms to others! My God!" Mani Mama exclaimed, wiping his head with his hand and looking sharply around!

The boxes were all marked, and the sweaters had some strange script, which the kids could not decipher. To their immense surprise, Mani could! He said it was the number '64' in Dogra Akkhar, an older form of the local language Dogri. Sixty-four, Daduji's house number! Anand remembered that Daduji had said theirs was the only house that was numbered so. But surely this was just sheer coincidence and the two were not connected? They were, however, impressed that Mani Mama was able to read this ancient script! What could he not do?

"Does this mean they're working from our house? Why is this number on these sweaters and what does this mean?" Manjari was the first to speak.

"The tunnel must lead somewhere *na*?" questioned Anjari. "But there isn't an opening like the one we entered just now in the house?"

The kids trembled with fear and were not sure if Mani Mama could handle all this, because usually, he was the first to panic in any situation. They were just about to walk further when they heard footsteps approaching them! They quickly turned around and tried to hide behind the crates. Was it the men coming back? And where were they coming from? It sounded like someone was descending a staircase. They peeped through the boxes, and to their shock, it was their own servant Khemu, and the knitter Asim Bhai! Asim Bhai? Here? So far from home? What was going on? The men spoke amongst themselves. The children couldn't make out what was being said. Mani Mama gestured to them to remain as quiet as mice.

They could hear Khemu's voice. *"Baddle baddle ... kharaa ... kharaa ..."*

Then Asim Bhai spoke. *"Traii ... Kalla ... kharaaa..."*

They caught only a few words and strained to understand what was being said! The men spoke for a few more minutes. The children couldn't understand a word of what was being said! They heard boxes being shuffled and then the footsteps seemed to become softer. It seemed like the men had left. They came out of hiding.

"Asim Bhai sounds like the leader," Mani Mama said. Abhay's eyes almost fell out of his head. Their soft-spoken knitter, with his heaps of wool and buttons and whatnot, was actually a terrorist dealing in arms!

Mani revealed that Khemu was just confirming to Asim Bhai that more boxes would arrive tomorrow. And that he would take care of everything. Asim Bhai told him that three more boxes needed to be delivered across the stream tomorrow! Khemu sounded anxious and assured Asim Bhai that everything would be fine. He shouldn't worry or get angry!

Things moved quickly once Mani Mama dropped this bomb on the kids! Mani Mama took a gadget out of his pocket and pressed a button. "I think we've got them. Tomorrow three more boxes move. Yes, it is the servant. And that wool supplier from Delhi is here too. You were right, the other end is the house."

Once again, the children were stumped. Mani saw their completely bewildered faces and explained. "Sorry for all the secrecy. I had to hide so much from you, and I didn't like it but that's a big part of my job."

Now the children looked even more confused. He was unemployed, no? The good-for-nothing Mani?

"I've been part of various secret service agencies and work for our government. I keep a low profile and pretend to be a loafer so as not to arouse suspicion," Mani explained.

"Daduji has known for a while now, but Ammaji and Phui don't know. The fewer people that know the safer it is for my assignments and family."

The children viewed Mani in a completely different light now!

"So, you knew about these sweater men?" Anjari asked wide-eyed.

"Well, we've been seeing a lot of illicit trade happening and are trying to track the goings on. We had to let a few deals go through as planned because we didn't want them to know we knew!" He looked tired.

The children looked at him in awe! Their very own James Bond!

"So then?" Abhay was keen to know more.

"Well, we now know the culprits because so far, these two were never seen. They probably meet and conduct all their dealings here in this tunnel and have others do the transporting."

"This tunnel leads to your Daduji's house Khemu just mentioned. I'm kind of flummoxed about where though. Your grandparents haven't been in that house for too long so I think these guys may have set this whole thing up much before, when it was empty for a few years between owners."

"So, what are we waiting for?" Anand was keen to continue.

"Yes, can we see where the tunnel leads to?" Manjari piped in.

Mani stood thinking.

"It may be okay, but the danger isn't completely gone. I do have men surrounding your Daduji's house as well as the entrance near the stream. Let's do this!"

The children excitedly followed Mani Mama and they walked for what seemed like another eternity. At one point in the tunnel, they had to crawl on all fours; the opening was so narrow. Suddenly, they came to a large room. It seemed to be very well-lit and looked well-used. They saw a metal ladder leading upwards. Mani motioned to the children to be quiet and wait. He gingerly climbed up the ladder.

"How could we have missed this!"

To their immense surprise, they found the ladder leading to Phui's bathroom! Mani Mama took out his gadget again and spoke into it. This time, the children couldn't understand a word of what he was saying!

"We did it!" He announced triumphantly!

"My team has caught the poor men transporting the crates. They hadn't reached far. Another couple is now escorting the family back. They are in for a surprise!" Mani Mama chuckled.

The children hadn't seen him this gleeful for as long as they had known him. He also explained to them that he had given orders to his men to march into the tunnel and confiscate all the crates. After a while, some men in plain clothes marched into the house. Khemu and Asim were with them and looked glum. They were in handcuffs. Mani came forward and the men in plain clothes saluted him. Khemu and Asim were surprised to see the whole gang, as Asim also recognized all of them.

Khemu admitted to using the tunnel leading into Phui's bathroom. It was convenient. It was always covered with a rug and they had conducted their business peacefully before Sr Mr Apte moved in. The children were certain that Phui was involved as well; it was her bathroom after all! She was probably involved to take revenge on Daduji as he had been the favourite of their parents. It all made sense. The children exchanged quick glances. Of course, they thought it was all rather disgusting, shameful and incredibly unbelievable!

Khemu showed them how he used the opening in the bathroom and covered it up afterwards. It was all very exciting, but the children were also shaken by everything that had taken place in the past two hours. They waited for the rest of the family to return so that Phui could be interrogated, and arrested. She was not their favourite! They also wanted to tell the whole family that their darling Mama was not the black sheep but the pride of the whole family. They eagerly waited for everyone to come home. They soon returned home and were surprised to see Mani Mama and the kids before them.

Phui, as usual, marched in frowning as she was not at all happy at being escorted back so hurriedly from the picnic. Mani took Phui aside saying that he wanted to talk to her, and she scowled at him angrily! The kids were too excited and spilt the beans about Mani. The elders were stunned. They tried to make sense of it all. Rajeshwari, Sukanya and Ammaji were in tears when they heard Mani was such a high-ranking officer. Daduji and his sons were shocked that there was a basement in the house and that a big criminal gang was working from there.

Phui was interrogated and asked about the connection between the gang and the basement opening from her bathroom. To everyone's surprise, she was ignorant of this development and didn't know about the opening! How dare they use her brother's house for such unscrupulous activities! Of course, she had spoken to that man that day. She had lambasted him because she thought he was the temporary cleaner Khemu had brought with him and had done a shoddy job cleaning her floors!

Mani and all the kids apologized to her, and she, for a change, looked happy and congratulated all of them, especially Mani Mama. She confessed how she had felt so bitter all her life because her brother was the centre of all the attention and love, but she realized now that those were things of the past and her attitude was only harming her and no one else! For the first time, they all saw a teary-eyed Phui, full of remorse. She held her arms wide, embraced all the kids and blessed Mani for his excellent work!

Soon everything was well in the Apte world. Mani and the police arrested all the smugglers and finally, **THE MYSTERY OF THE KNITTED SWEATER** was solved.

The tunnel was sealed with a cement wall, and now it was just a basement for the family, for which there was a separate entrance from the backyard.

The kids enjoyed the rest of their holidays with the family. Mani was promoted for his excellent work and the kids were lauded and appreciated for their courage. Mani got busy with another case, but that of course is another story! Rajeshwari and her parents were proud of him.

Soon it was time to bid adieu and return to their homes and school. It was a very teary and sad day for the family, especially the children who had had such an adventurous vacation! Daduji, Ammaji, and to everyone's surprise, Phui, came to the station to see them off. Amidst promises to visit again and of course write long letters, the children said their goodbyes. The train soon left the platform and the kids waved goodbye to the trio, who were in tears, taking back with them the adventurous memories of the vacation.

The Mystery of the Blue Sapphire

Summer vacation had begun, and the three children, Charu, Tanay and Sahil were very excited. They lived in Shivpuri, a town in Madhya Pradesh. Their father, Balwant Singh, was a collector and their mother, Leela, was a loving wife and doting mother.

"Where are we going for our vacation, Ma?" Charu asked.

"Nowhere," replied Leela. "No!" cried all the children in disappointment.

"But...your Bhua and cousin Kalyan are coming here for the holidays!" smiled their mother with a twinkle in her eyes.

"Yeah!" the children shouted with happiness.

Upon hearing this, Nani frowned; she was not fond of Arti or Kalyan. "Poor Leela will have to do so much more work once they arrive," Nani muttered to the children.

"Amma, whenever Arti comes, you make that poor girl do your bidding, and you still crib! But don't worry, you won't have to give Arti or Kalyan anything when they leave." Leela laughed.

Nani lived with Leela, as she was her only child. Nani was very stingy, unlike her daughter who welcomed her sister-in-law and her son Kalyan, who was great company for her three children.

Charu was the eldest, a petite girl, very shy and extremely intelligent. She was fair, with hazel eyes and a rosy complexion. Tanay was younger than Charu, but she always treated her like a younger sister. He was tall, dusky and rather intelligent. He could speak to anyone with confidence. Sahil was the baby of the whole household. He had curly hair like his father, was fair and very mischievous; he was not interested in studying.

They were all very fond of Bhua and Kalyan, who were almost the same age as Tanay. There was just a week left before their arrival, and a lot of preparations had to be done. The children were full of ideas.

Leela got busy in the kitchen, baking cakes, and making a variety of biscuits and other goodies which Kalyan relished. Nani did not approve of all this; she thought it was a waste of money and unnecessary hard work for her poor daughter.

"Leela, why take so much trouble for Arti and that brat? Buy some cheap biscuits and a cake from the market for them," she complained said.

"Amma, I love doing all this for them. Arti is such a sweetheart, and Kalyan is a little darling, NOT a brat. The children are so fond of him and their aunt. She is my only sister-in-law, and we are her only close relatives. After Naren's death, we should take care of her." Leela got busy mixing the batter for the cake.

"Do not entertain her for more than a week. How long is she coming for?" Nani asked Leela, irritated.

Leela mischievously smiled at her mother and said, "Oh, I don't know, about two months, or maybe more," teased Leela. "It's after all her own brother's house."

"HEY RAM!" Nani exclaimed.

Balwant was unaware of the hustle and bustle going on in their house. He was a quiet, shy person…tall, dark, and according to his wife, not handsome. Poor guy, it was the tragedy of his life that his dear wife, who, though she was madly in love with him, thought that his looks were not one of his plusses! He was extremely fond of his children. Both his sons thought that he was partial to Charu. When he returned home that evening, Leela gave him the good news of his sister's arrival. He never expressed himself, but upon hearing this, he smiled and said it would be a good change for Choti, his sister.

"What are you planning to give Choti this time?" Balwant asked his wife.

"I've asked Ramniklal to make a gold chain for her. I hope she likes it," she said excitedly. Ramniklal was the only jeweller in town, and he was famous for his collection of rare jewels.

There were only two days left for the much-awaited arrival of their aunt and cousin, and the threesome had gone to buy some stuff for their mother. On the way back home, they noticed that Kanta dadi had still not returned after meeting her grandson Kalu, who lived and worked in the neighbouring town.

Kanta dadi was an old lady who lived alone. The entire town knew her and was very fond of her, especially the three children and their cousin Kalyan. She often went to the next town to meet her grandson, who was much older than the four children. They did not like him much.

Soon, Bhua and Kalyan arrived and the whole house was filled with laughter and chatter. Arti was short, fair and an extrovert, unlike her elder brother. Kalyan was tall and dark-complexioned with exceptionally thick eyelashes. Finally, the four of them were together, and once more it was time for a whale of a time!

Arti and Leela became very busy at once chatting about old times. They got along very well. It was a happy time for everyone except Nani, who thought God was being unfair to her dear daughter.

The children would wake up early in the morning, go for long walks, horse riding and boating in the nearby river; it was all great fun.

One evening, when they were returning home after a walk, they saw light in Kanta dadi's cottage. They wondered who it could be. Dadi couldn't have returned already, could she? They were all curious and knocked on the door. The door opened and an old lady stood there smiling.

"Oh, Dadi!" Charu exclaimed, "You're back!"

"Yes, my babies, how have you all been?" Dadi asked, fondly.

"Oh! We missed you a lot, dadi," Sahil said, returning the affection and hugging her. He was the baby of the foursome.

"Hmm! Did you really miss me, or my goodies?" Dadi teasingly asked the children. She knew Charu, Tanay, Sahil and Kalyan were very fond of her homemade jams and pickles with puris.

"Here, I've made some fruit jam for all of you," she said, smiling affectionately.

"Yippy! Dadi, you're the best!" The children were overjoyed, and they all hugged her at once, nearly knocking her down.

"Oh dear, oh dear, come on now, take it and run along home, I would like to rest now, okay?"

"Bye, *dadi,*" the children cried in unison and set off for home.

They were thrilled about dadi's return and came home and told Leela and Arti about it.

"Oh! That old hag is back," Nani scowled, while the children ignored her comment totally and went off to the kitchen to find something to have with the jam.

The next morning, the police came to Balwant Singh's house to give them some news.

"We have some shocking and strange news."

They all wondered what it could be.

"Ramniklal is MISSING, and the very rare blue sapphire can't be found. His family has no clue, and that wife of his won't stop crying," the officer informed them.

They were all shocked.

"But I met him just the other day. How can he be missing today?" Leela wondered aloud.

Who? When? How? Everybody had several questions. No one had a clue.

The police would give them no more details.

The townsfolk were a bit tense and scared; such a thing had never happened before. Where had he gone? Would he return? Had he been kidnapped? What about the jewels? Had he taken it with him? Or was it stolen?

Was he okay? What happened? No one knew. They only hoped to find out soon.

The Singh household was extremely tense because Balwant was the collector and even though this wasn't entirely his jurisdiction, he did a lot for the town and in turn, everyone turned to him to figure out what had happened.

That evening, Kanta dadi called on them and brought some homemade pickles.

"Oh, dadi, you really shouldn't have," Leela protested, though she too loved dadi's goodies.

"Arre, I heard that Ramniklal is missing. They say he's been kidnapped. I wonder who's kidnapped that stingy fool," *dadi* said.

"Maybe, it's because of that rare gemstone which he had bought a few days ago. He was very excited and talked about it incessantly when he had come home the other day to deliver the gold chain I had ordered," Leela told dadi.

"Chalo, whatever happened was destined, it's God's will. Everything happens for the best." Saying this, dadi left.

"Ma, why is dadi so insensitive and inhuman at times?" Tanay asked Leela.

"I don't know if she's insensitive, but people of that generation seem to leave a lot to fate and resign things to God's will. And, my dear, you know the tragedy that struck the poor lady. Her son and daughter-in-law were killed, so she behaves slightly odd sometimes. Never mind her, put these in the kitchen, and NO, you can't have any of it just now," Leela gently chided her son.

Some days passed by, but Balwant and his officers were unable to resolve the case. It was quite frustrating for everyone. Then, one night they were almost asleep when they heard horses' hoofs.

Tanay thought aloud, "Who could it be this late at night?"

"Silly, it must be Kalu; only he would ride a horse at a time when everyone has wheels! He's probably brought his friends along to show them our beautiful town and treat them to dadi's yummy food," Charu told her younger brother.

"Try and sleep now, we'll go to dadi's house tomorrow and find out."

Tanay was not convinced. This did not seem to be normal, something was amiss; maybe dadi's life was in danger. She was old and stayed alone, a little away from the others. A little excited, he told Charu and Kalyan to change so that they could check in on her.

"Please, I won't be able to get any sleep, let's go see now, come on, both of you have always wanted adventure, now's our chance!" Tanay pleaded.

"Okay. People riding horses late in the evening is not a reason to be suspicious. Really! You've been reading too many mystery comics! I'm not really looking for an adventure, but I'm not very sleepy, so let's go!" Charu said, getting out of bed.

Sahil was fast asleep and was not fond of going out at night since he feared darkness.

The children came out of their rooms, and saw Nani frowning at them suspiciously. "Where are you all going? Come on, go to bed." She had woken up to have her midnight medicine.

"Nani, we are just going downstairs to read in the living room. Better light," Charu told her.

Thankfully, she was not wearing her spectacles, so she could not see that they were not in their nightclothes. They quickly collected two torches and some water. They came out of the house. It was a clear, starry night and it seemed that the whole town was asleep. They could hear the trees swaying and jackals crying. Charu was quite scared but dared not express her fear, as Tanay would give her a lecture on how she should be brave. They came closer to dadi's house and could see the lights on. Yes, Kalu had just come. As they neared the house gates, they saw six horses standing in the compound.

"So Kalu has got some friends over," Tanay told Charu and Kalyan.

They could hear voices coming from the house. They were keen to discretely see what was happening inside. There was a window on one side of the living room. They went towards the window and peeped inside. They saw six men, including Kalu, seated around dadi. But surprisingly, they all had rifles. Was dadi in some danger? They all looked terrifying. Was Kalu involved with some gang, they wondered.

Charu, sounding a little worried, said, "Poor dadi, I hope this is not as scary as it looks."

"Oh, look! See what's happening!" They almost choked seeing dadi remove her white hair.

"It's a wig," whispered an excited Tanay to a shocked Kalyan. She had jet-black hair underneath the wig!

She slowly took off what was a mask, revealing a very young face. It did not look at all like the old dadi they knew and loved.

"Oh, God!" They almost screamed!

"Our dadi is the famous notorious dacoit, Hirabai," Charu said.

Yes, she was Hirabai. Fierce-looking eyes, red henna-coloured hair, chewing paan, and absolutely straight-backed. Dadi's hunchback had vanished. In the quiet night, they could hear that her voice was crisp, not a sign of old age. The children were in a state of shock. Their thinking power had gone, their minds went blank.

Charu was almost in tears. Tanay and Kalyan were trying to be brave but had never felt more scared in their entire young lives. For five minutes they were totally shaken and numb with shock.

Suddenly, they returned to their senses; they heard Hirabai saying that they had to leave before sunrise. The children had read about Hirabai and her gang in the newspapers and from their father. They also knew she had a romantic partner, another well-known dacoit, Kali Singh.

Charu was the first to speak, and said, "Now it all makes sense. Our dadi is Hirabai and Kalu is no grandson but her lover, Kali Singh, the famed dacoit."

Hirabai's name figured at the top of the most-wanted list of the police in the country. There was also a huge prize for anyone who could catch her, dead or alive.

Tanay whispered to the other two. "We should get home as fast as we can and inform Pa about all this."

As they turned, Charu's sharp eye caught something gleaming in the hut. She strained to see what it was and leaned in a little.

"Oh my God!" she nearly lost her balance.

"That's the blue sapphire everyone was talking about! On dadi's, I mean Hirabai's neck! Look!" she whispered to the other two, who were trying hard to catch a glimpse of this rare jewel, without being seen.

It was on Hirabai's neck, strung on a black thread. The pale blue jewel was exotic. Even from a distance, they could see the sparkle.

"Which means she knows where Ramniklal is?" Kalyan said.

"This is getting even more exciting! A real adventure." Tanay could barely keep his voice down. Kalyan suggested they go home and get Balwant Singh and the police here before Hirabai escaped.

"Let's take off our slippers so we don't make any noise and leave," Charu, the wise one, said.

The children hurried out of the gate and walked as fast as they could, their legs still shaking, afraid that if caught they'd all be dead. They were all convinced that Hirabai had kidnapped Ramniklal and stolen the jewel. Where could Ramniklal be? That was the million-dollar question. There was no place in that small cottage. They finally reached the gates of their house and heaved a sigh of relief.

Soon, the whole household was awake, except for little Sahil. The children narrated the whole incident to their elders.

"So, Dadi is Hirabai!" exclaimed Leela, with a tinge of sadness in her voice, as she had grown very fond of dadi over the five years she had lived in Shivpuri.

Hirabai, together with that wretched Kali Singh, had fooled the entire town.

Nani scowled and said, "I've always told you all to stay away from that lady, you people never listened to me."

Balwant consoled her saying, "Yes, Amma. You were right for once."

Soon, Balwant Singh informed the police and issued orders to catch Hirabai and the gang red-handed.

"But, uncle, where is Ramniklal?" Kalyan asked worriedly.

"We'll find out once we arrest her," Balwant assured his nephew.

Arti and Leela fondly looked at their children, proud of their achievements.

Balwant Singh was ready to arrest Hirabai and her gang. The children insisted that since they had helped in solving the mystery of the blue sapphire, they would like to accompany him. Balwant readily agreed to their request.

Sunrise was only two hours away. As Balwant and the kids reached the cottage, the police also arrived. They were well-armed and had circled the cottage from all sides; there was no chance of any escape. They were just in time since the gang was about to leave.

As soon as Hirabai opened the door, what did she see? There were armed policemen all around, and the inspector with his pistol had blocked her way. With the entire police force there, she could not escape. Hirabai and her gang were caught. They were handcuffed, and without any fuss, they surrendered with their handcuffed hands up and rifles behind their heads. She angrily looked at the children who peeped from the jeep.

Balwant asked Hirabai, "Where have you kept Ramniklal?"

She kept mum. The police inspector slapped her hard and threatened to hit her more if she didn't disclose his whereabouts.

To their shock, she said, "He's here! Down in the basement."

On hearing this, Charu fainted. She could not handle this anymore.

"Pata nahin kis chakki ka atta khata hai, mara nahin," Hirabai said in anger.

(I don't know what he's made of, he's still alive!)

There was a basement in this small cottage; this shocked the children. The two boys, along with four policemen, went down to the basement from the kitchen. They found Ramniklal tied and gagged. He was semi-conscious and badly bruised, poor guy. He was immediately taken to the hospital.

Meanwhile, Charu had regained consciousness and was feeling better.

The mystery was finally solved. The children were jubilant!

Later, Ramniklal, in his statement to the police, said that Kali Singh had stolen the sapphire and kidnapped him.

The next day, the children were the talk of the town. The whole town was proud of their bravery and courage. Never in the history of this sleepy town had there been so much excitement. They were also given a prize of Rs 50,000, the reward for catching Hirabai.

All is well that ends well. Nani finally appreciated Kalyan and tried to be large-hearted and gave him Rs 50, a huge amount for someone as stingy as her!

The summer holidays came to an end. Bhua and Kalyan left amidst a tearful farewell.

"Come soon," Tanay shouted as the train left, and Kalyan smiled and yelled back, "Next vacation, more adventures! See you soon!"

THE END

www.ingramcontent.com/pod-product-compliance
Lightning Source LLC
La Vergne TN
LVHW041043150826
845672LV00001B/441

9798889359517